Jane confuses the hell out of me. Maybe it will help to write out my objectives. I'm not used to putting anything on paper, but I can always destroy this later.

Objectives Attained:
1. Quit the Agency
2. Activate Samuel Charmaneaux identity
3. Find Jane Smith

Objectives Remaining:
1. Find an ordinary job
2. Make a place for myself in my new hometown
3. Marry Jane

The first two objectives depend on the last one. Jane doesn't like risks, so I have to make her either need me or want me enough to take a chance. I don't understand what she wants from me, or what happens to me when I kiss her, but I know she wants me—almost as much as I want her. I can use that to get her to agree to marry me.

New objective: Seduce Jane.

Dear Reader,

Welcome to Silhouette Desire—where you're guaranteed powerful, passionate and provocative love stories that feature rugged heroes and spirited heroines who experience the full emotional intensity of falling in love!

Wonderful and ever-popular Annette Broadrick brings us September's MAN OF THE MONTH with *Lean, Mean & Lonesome*. Watch as a tough loner returns home to face the woman he walked away from but never forgot.

Our exciting continuity series TEXAS CATTLEMAN'S CLUB continues with *Cinderella's Tycoon* by Caroline Cross. Charismatic CEO Sterling Churchill marries a shy librarian pregnant with his sperm-bank baby—and finds love.

Proposition: Marriage is what rising star Eileen Wilks offers when the girl-next-door comes alive in the arms of an alpha hero. Beloved romance author Fayrene Preston makes her Desire debut with *The Barons of Texas: Tess,* featuring a beautiful heiress who falls in love with a sexy stranger. The popular theme BACHELORS & BABIES returns to Desire with Metsy Hingle's *Dad in Demand*. And Barbara McCauley's miniseries SECRETS! continues with the dramatic story of a mysterious millionaire in *Killian's Passion.*

So make a commitment to sensual love—treat yourself to all six September love stories from Silhouette Desire!

Enjoy!

Joan Marlow Golan
Senior Editor, Silhouette Desire

Please address questions and book requests to:
Silhouette Reader Service
U.S.: 3010 Walden Ave., P.O. Box 1325, Buffalo, NY 14269
Canadian: P.O. Box 609, Fort Erie, Ont. L2A 5X3

PROPOSITION: MARRIAGE
EILEEN WILKS

SILHOUETTE *Desire*®
Published by Silhouette Books
America's Publisher of Contemporary Romance

SILHOUETTE BOOKS

ISBN 0-373-76239-9

PROPOSITION: MARRIAGE

Visit us at www.romance.net

Printed in U.S.A.

Books by Eileen Wilks

Silhouette Desire

The Loner and the Lady #1008
The Wrong Wife #1065
Cowboys Do It Best #1109
Just a Little Bit Pregnant #1134
Just a Little Bit Married? #1188
Proposition: Marriage #1239

Silhouette Intimate Moments

The Virgin and the Outlaw #857
Midnight Cinderella #921

EILEEN WILKS

is a fifth-generation Texan. Her great-great-grandmother came to Texas in a covered wagon shortly after the end of the Civil War—excuse us, the War Between the States. But she's not a full-blooded Texan. Right after another war, her Texan father fell for a Yankee woman. This obviously mismatched pair proceeded to travel to nine cities in three countries in the first twenty years of their marriage. For the next twenty years they stayed put, back home in Texas again—and still together.

Eileen figures her professional career matches her nomadic upbringing, since she's tried everything from drafting to a brief stint as a ranch hand—raising two children and any number of cats and dogs along the way. Not until she started writing did she "stay put," because that's when she knew she'd come home. Readers can write to her at P.O. Box 4612, Midland, TX 79704-4612.

This book is dedicated to my bookseller friends—
to Sherry at Miz B's for her support, her friendship
and for many, many hours of reading pleasure;
to Rick at Waldenbooks for always going the extra yard;
and to Donita Lawrence at Bell, Book and Candle for her
loving support of romance books, romance writers
and romance readers everywhere.

One

Repentance came too late. Jane was up to her neck in lake water and trouble.

The lake was a shallow one. The trouble waited about ten feet away, in the form of a pair of combat boots planted right at her eye level on the muddy bank. Jane crouched behind a bush that clung to life in spite of its recent inundation, and wished very hard for the impossible.

She wished she'd never heard of the small Caribbean nation of San Tomás. She wished even more that she hadn't bought the cruise tickets a fellow teacher had been forced to sell when his wife's appendix ruptured just before spring break. Most of all, she wished she'd never given in to the rare spirit of adventure that had moved her to leave the port city where the cruise ship was docked, and go haring off to investigate the island's interior.

Why, oh why, had she decided to toss aside the cautious habits of a lifetime and live a little?

The boots belonged to a soldier. The soldier had one friend

nearby, whom she couldn't see through her bush, and others spread out in the surrounding tropical forest. All were looking for her, and they had guns—big, mean-looking, Rambo-type guns.

The water was warm, the air was still and hot, but Jane shivered.

Until she'd heard the gunshots, she had been enjoying herself tremendously. She'd made several friends on the bus, including a native couple who had told her proudly about the dam the government had built nearby. Jane was sure she was more profoundly grateful for that dam than anyone else could be. Especially for the newness of it. That dam had created the shallow lake where she crouched. Its waters had swallowed part of the forest and killed off the ground-hugging plants, but it hadn't finished drowning the trees and larger bushes. Jane's bush still had plenty of leaves to hide behind.

Though she couldn't see the soldiers' faces now, she'd seen them in the village before she'd fled. They had all looked terribly young to her—no older than most of the boys she taught back home in Atherton. She'd noticed the dozen-or-so youthful soldiers with wicked-looking rifles slung over bony shoulders as soon as she'd climbed off the bus, but she hadn't thought anything of it. Not really. Soldiers were a common sight in San Tomás.

Everything had happened so fast. When the bus driver had announced they had to stop for repairs, she hadn't minded because she'd needed to find a ladies' room. Seconds after she went into a local cantina, a boy she had met on the bus had come running in. He'd tried to warn her, but she hadn't believed him—not until she'd been washing her hands in the tiny rest room, and had heard gunfire.

She'd crawled out the narrow window and had run for her life. The dirt path she'd stumbled across had led her straight to this lake, and her bush.

"Hernández is a fool," one of the soldiers said in Spanish. "Do you see a woman? Of course not, because she isn't here.

Why would anyone head this way, right into the lake? Even a silly *norteamericana* would not be such a fool. But even if we find her, what good will it do us? Will any of that ransom he talks about find its way into our pockets?''

The other soldier chuckled and made a crude comment about what Hernández could do with his orders. The first young man laughed.

Whom had they been shooting at, back at the village? Jane tried not to think about that. It made her shiver, and she didn't want to move, not even a breath. But it was hard, very hard, to be still.

There was a bug on her hand. It had climbed on when she'd gripped one limb of the bush—another move that she repented too late, because now she didn't dare move her hand to release the bush. *They* might hear.

The bug was a huge, horrid monster of an insect as long as her little finger. It sat on her hand and stared at her, its carapace shining greenish-black in the sun, and it had too many legs. That was how bugs were. They had all those squirmy little legs. Jane purely hated being touched by squirmy little bug-legs.

Jane stared at the bug while she listened to the obscene joke the first soldier told, and to the second soldier's laughter. Her other hand—the bugless one—gripped a tiny locket that hung on a chain around her neck. The two young men argued about where each of them would search for her.

Then they talked about what they would do if they found her.

When she heard one of them leaving, she waited for the tight band of terror around her chest to ease. It didn't.

They'd just been talking tough to impress each other, she told herself. In spite of the guns, they were just kids—kids the same age as the ones she taught Spanish to, back at Atherton High, for heaven's sake. They'd been talking about things they didn't understand. Surely they couldn't understand the reality of what they had said they would do to her.

Fear nearly choked her. The edge of the little disk she wore around her neck dug into the pads of her fingers, nearly cutting the skin. Papa, she thought, why did you always tell me I was like you? I'm not. I'm not cut out for adventures.

She wondered what had happened to the other foreigners who'd been on the bus. Please, God, she prayed, let them be all right. That German couple had been so nice, and so had the other passengers—like the quietly gorgeous man with the wire-rimmed glasses who had sat in the bench seat across from her. Jane couldn't stand to think that the gunfire she'd heard had been directed at him. She'd talked with many of the others on the bus, but hadn't gotten up the nerve to speak to him.

Normally, Jane made friends easily. That was one advantage to being unremarkable. She might secretly long for one outstanding trait, good or bad, but people did relax with her because she was so very average. New acquaintances often said she reminded them of someone—a niece, a friend from school, the daughter of a neighbor.

But something about the man she'd mentally dubbed "the professor" had made her uncharacteristically uncertain. Maybe it was the East Coast look of him, with those trendy glasses and baggy chinos, that had intimidated her. He'd seemed rather reserved, but she'd decided he was probably shy.

And his hands… For some reason, his hands had fascinated her. He'd had big hands, curiously graceful, with long, elegant fingers, yet she'd seen a number of small nicks and scrapes such as a workingman collects. She'd been downright silly about his hands, in fact, letting them feature in a mildly sexual fantasy. It had been perfectly safe to fantasize, of course. He hadn't noticed her. Men seldom did.

What had happened to him? she wondered now. If the guerrillas were looking for hostages to ransom, surely they wouldn't have hurt any of the foreigners on the bus.

Ten feet from her bush, the army boots moved.

The bug decided to move, too, tickling her hand with its squirmy feet. Jane grimaced. It was hard to hold still with a monster bug strolling around on her arm.

She couldn't see what Army Boots was doing, not through the shrubbery, but her ears told her he hadn't gone far. She heard the scritch of a match being struck and smelled sulfur. For one panicked moment she thought he was going to burn her bush down, then the scent of tobacco smoke drifted her way, making her feel foolish. He'd stopped to light a cigarette, of course, not to commit arson upon her hiding place. He stood there smoking it about fifteen feet from where she crouched, sodden and scared.

The bug paused, waved its fuzzy antennae at her, and rounded the bend of her elbow.

So far, this was shaping up to be one hell of a vacation.

Cinnamon trees mingled with kapok, yellow cedar, mahoe and boxwood in the tropical forest. Some of the trees would die over the next year, their roots or trunks rotted away by the new lake. The big mango tree sitting several feet back from the northern edge of the water would probably survive.

The man perched in that tree had a lot in common with it. Few of the locals realized that mangoes weren't native to the island. Mango trees had been around long enough and had adapted readily enough that it didn't occur to anyone that they didn't belong. Like the tree, the man was a survivor. Like it, he was good at fitting into places where he didn't belong. He rested comfortably in a vee formed by the trunk and a thick branch, and watched the woman and the soldiers.

The newly-formed lake was, for him, a mixed blessing. The woman had found a place to hide, which was good. But water covered the dirt track he'd planned to take to his pickup spot on the other side of the island. Not so good.

The situation had changed. He had some decisions to make.

The mango tree did a better job of hiding him than the

woman's bush did for her. He could keep track of the ragged
soldado from Ruiz's so-called Liberation Army who stood
smoking a cigarette some twenty feet to the west. He also
had a decent view of the woman in the lake. Her pale sundress floated out around her in the muddy water, making her
easy to spot.

She looked pretty pathetic. Even her hair was dispirited—
a dark, dripping cap plastered to her head.

But he'd seen her hair when it was dry. Dry, it held fire
hidden in its depths, a richness that only showed when sunlight struck sparks off it. On the bus, he'd watched her. His
life sometimes depended on how well he observed those
around him, so he'd taken note of all the passengers, including the cheerful American tourist who had chatted with the
others in surprisingly good Spanish.

Maybe he had rested his eyes on her more than was strictly
necessary. She was so very American, so blessedly ordinary.
It had soothed him to look at her. Of course, her hair wasn't
ordinary at all, though it pretended to be. Such a warm brown
it was, and thick enough to make a man's hands itch to touch
it.

He shook his head. Silly woman. She was clutching her
bush as if it made her invisible. Couldn't she tell that as soon
as the soldier moved east along the shore of the little lake
he'd be able to see her?

Probably not. Few people saw the world accurately, and
she was a civilian. Her only experience of hiding had probably ended when she and her friends had stopped waiting to
hear ''Ally, ally, outs in free,'' and had started playing kissing games.

The thought of playing kissing games with the woman
snagged his attention for one surprising second. He remembered the way she'd laughed on the bus. She'd been talking
to that boy, the one he'd bribed to warn her of the guerrillas'
plans. She had a warm laugh, as warm and inviting as her
hair.

He'd thought of kissing her then—when she'd laughed.

The *soldado* threw down his cigarette butt and shouldered his rifle. He started moving east.

The woman didn't move. She stayed put—poor, foolish creature, huddled up to her armpits in lake water, hiding behind her bush. He doubted she could see the man who was looking for her. She didn't realize the guerrilla would be in a position to see her soon.

It didn't matter, he told himself. What he'd learned about the ties being formed between two terrorist groups would affect the lives of a great many more women than this one. If she were caught—no, *when* she was caught, he amended, because she obviously would be—she shouldn't suffer too much. Ruiz was after ransom, and the self-styled *generalissimo* wasn't a vicious man; he would have no need or intention of harming his hostages. The woman might have a rough couple of weeks, but she should be okay. Ruiz didn't want to look like a barbarian in the press. He just wanted money.

Only…Ruiz wasn't a real general. He wasn't even a real soldier, though he wore a fancy uniform and quoted Che Guevara. His control over his troops was poor, and, while some of his soldiers were as decent as men in their positions could be, others gave beasts a bad name.

If the woman were raped, he thought, she wouldn't laugh that warm laugh anymore. Not for a very long time.

Maybe not ever.

It had nothing to do with him, he reminded himself; nothing to do with his purpose for being here. He'd seen that she received a warning. He'd even lingered after sending that warning, hoping to see that she'd gotten safely away. There was nothing more he could do without risking himself inexcusably.

He told himself these things, but his hands were already moving to find the grips he needed to climb out on a limb for a wet, frightened woman.

The bug was three inches past Jane's elbow when she heard a thud—a sudden, solid thud, as if something heavy had fallen on the nearby shore.

She jumped. Her arm moved, the branch jerked, the leaves rustled and the bug fell into the water.

There was a grunt and a dull smack. A *hitting* sort of smack. After seven years as a teacher and twenty-nine years as a sister to two quarrelsome brothers, she knew that sound. She swallowed the whimper trying to climb out of her throat and crab-walked backward, sure she had to get away. Her wet dress clung to her legs, hampering her movement.

She paused, still crouched low. Now she couldn't hear anything. Even the birds were quiet. That stupid bug was swimming toward her, and she had no idea where the soldier was, what was going on, or what she should do. Jane was used to being sensible, but common sense wasn't much help in such an utterly uncommon situation. So she stayed where she was, frozen by indecision, straining to hear.

What was that? Behind her—

Before she could turn, a hand clamped over her mouth.

Panic sent her heartbeat into triple time. She tried to bite the hand, but long fingers dug into her cheeks and she couldn't get her mouth open. The hand jerked her head back. She took a deep, panicked breath through her nose and inhaled her attacker's scent just as his other arm wrapped around her. He forced her off-balance so that she knelt, water lapping at her breasts, with her upper body bent awkwardly back. The hand on her mouth kept her head tilted, exposing her neck.

She thought about necks and knives. Nausea mixed with the panicked drumming of her heart.

A voice spoke in her ear in tiny puffs of air, softer than a whisper. "The soldier with the cigarette is unconscious, but there's another one in the trees to the west. He'll hear us if we make any noise. Are you going to scream if I take my hand off your mouth?"

He spoke English. American English. Relief made her limp, and she managed to shake her head in spite of the brutal grip of his hand.

At last that hand left her mouth, though his arm stayed wrapped around her. She held her breath, trying to reassure him with her silence that she had the sense to be very, very quiet.

When he let go, she nearly toppled over backward. His hand on her shoulder steadied her. Taking care not to splash, she stood, turned—and almost forgot the need for silence.

His glasses were gone. Everything else was the same—the loose white shirt, baggy chinos, and straight brown hair pulled back in a ponytail—but the glasses were gone, and with them had gone the man who'd worn them. It was the eyes, she thought. Those cold, blue-as-heaven eyes meeting hers didn't belong to a shy professor. No. The man standing in front of her now, his pants wet from the thighs down, was something else; something so far outside her experience, she couldn't put a label on him. She stood, mute and shaken, staring at the stranger in front of her.

He held a finger to his lips in the age-old gesture for quiet, and she realized his hands were the same. The same long fingers and palms, the same calluses and small nicks. Even though the man was different, the hands were the same. It was absurdly reassuring.

She nodded her understanding.

He turned.

She started to follow, but paused, looking down at the water that came up to her thighs now that she was on her feet. The bug was still swimming valiantly, but it was confused. It was going in circles. She hesitated, but for only a second. The stupid thing was going to drown itself.

Quickly she scooped up the horrid creature, using the hand it had already touched. Ugh. Bug legs. Her face scrunched up in disgust, she dumped the glistening monster-bug onto the relative safety of her bush, and turned.

The man who was not a professor had stopped five feet away. He stared at her, an odd expression on his face. He probably wanted to ask if she was nuts. That was what Doug used to ask her whenever she did something he thought was dumb, which had happened rather often in the last couple of months of their ill-fated engagement.

She shrugged apologetically and tried a smile. It hurt her cheek.

He didn't smile back. He turned and started for the shore— the western shore, which made no sense to her. He'd said there was another soldier in those woods, so why was he going that way?

Because she had no idea what else to do, she followed him.

Jane felt as frightened and confused as the bug must have been when it swam in circles, looking for land. She wanted to cry. On the one hand, she wanted the boyish professor back. An odd pang of loss assailed her over a man who had never existed. Yet she had to admit that the person she'd thought existed behind those gold-framed glasses wouldn't have known what to do in this situation. This man, with his cold blue eyes and elegant hands, apparently did.

They reached the drowning trees first, then the muddy shore. He gestured at her, indicating he wanted her to hide behind one of the larger trees and wait.

She shook her head. The safety he offered was precarious, but at least he knew what to do. Jane hated not knowing what to do even more than she hated bugs. So she smiled and refused silently, but the smile made her face hurt where his long fingers had dug into her flesh.

She had actually fantasized about those hands. Her face heated when she remembered that. To her dismay, the rest of her body heated, too.

He moved quickly, startling a gasp out of her, stopping so close to her that she could feel the heat from his body all up and down her own wet, too-aware flesh. One strand of his hair had come loose from his ponytail, and it tickled her neck when he bent his head. ''I have to take out the other *soldado*,'' he whispered so softly she scarcely heard him, even with his lips brushing her ear. His breath was as gentle and warm as his words were cold. ''I'd rather not kill him. It will be easier to avoid that if you aren't trotting along behind me.''

She swallowed, nodded, and went to wait behind the tree he'd indicated. And she tried to convince herself that her goose bumps came from fear, or from being wet. From anything except the remembered thrill of his lips brushing her ear.

Two

The second soldier was as easy to surprise as the first one had been. The watcher came up behind his quarry, silent as a shadow, and locked his forearm across the *soldado's* throat, his right hand finding the carotid artery with deadly speed. His victim didn't struggle long. Cutting off the blood flow to the brain was a faster way of knocking a man out than trying to throttle him, and a good deal quieter and more certain than hitting him over the head.

After seven carefully counted seconds, he lowered the unconscious body to the ground, then lightly felt the artery again. He held his breath, then let it out, relieved, as soon as he felt the pulse.

Killing some poor SOB accidentally would have been a hell of a note on which to end his career with the agency.

It took only a moment to use the man's belt to tie his arms behind him. That wouldn't hold him for long, but they couldn't expect a long delay, anyhow. There were other searchers, and not all of them were Ruiz's poorly trained, poorly equipped guerrillas.

Not all of them were after the woman, either.

He straightened and looked down at his victim, who wasn't really a man at all, he saw. Not yet, anyway. Sixteen or seventeen, at a guess. Scarcely old enough to grow a beard. Had soldiers always been so painfully young? Or was he getting old?

Of course, he was himself capable of looking both young and innocent, though he couldn't remember being the former, and wasn't sure he'd ever been the latter. It was a useful skill, but he doubted he could manage it if he were the one unconscious.

He made his silent way back to where he'd left the woman. She was peering around the trunk of the tree, looking in the wrong direction. Her gauzy sundress had originally been long and loose and white; it was still long, dragging about her ankles, but now it was wet and dirty and nearly transparent. He had a marvelous view of her rounded rump and white bikini panties beneath the clinging fabric.

He smiled and gave in to a rare impulse. "Boo," he said conversationally.

She jumped half a mile.

He had his impulses under control and his smile tucked back out of sight by the time she spun around. She was really kind of cute, even half-drowned as she was right now; small and cute and round all over, like a kitten. Her face was round and innocent. Her body was nicely rounded, too, if not so innocent looking, with plenty of curves and softness in just the places where a man liked to find curves and softness. Even her big brown eyes were round at the moment.

Then they narrowed. "You scared me on purpose. I take it the other soldier is, uh—unconscious?"

He shrugged dismissively. Let her wonder what he'd done. It might make her jump more quickly when he wanted her to jump. "There's no one close enough to hear us at the moment." They needed to put some distance between them and Ruiz's men while they could. He turned away. "Come on."

"Where?"

He headed for his mango tree.

"Dang it," she said. The rubbery squish of wet tennis shoes hurried along behind him. "Where are we going?"

"To get my gear, first." He reached the tree, crouched, and jumped, catching the lowest branch. He heaved himself up.

"Then what happens?" She tilted her head back, watching him.

"We go to a village I know about on the old Camino Real—that's the royal highway."

"I *know* what it means. What I want to know is—"

"That's right, you speak Spanish, don't you? I hope we can reach the village before dark, but I'm not sure of the route. Between Ruiz's troops and the new lake, my choices have become limited." He grabbed his backpack from the crotch of the tree. "Watch out." He tossed it down.

She jumped back just in time.

He swung down to land beside her. The sight of her from the front was just as appealing as it had been from behind. A little gold locket lay in the valley formed by full, pretty breasts. Her lacy white bra kept him from seeing as much of her nipples as he would have liked, but he could see their shadows beneath the two layers of wet cloth.

It was probably just as well she had on the bra, he decided. The low hum of arousal he felt now was pleasant. More would be distracting.

Either she liked letting him look, or she was too upset to realize how transparent her dress was. "But the old Camino Real is in the high country to the east," she said earnestly. "Shouldn't we head south, back where we came from? Or west? There's a decent-size town to the west—Narista, I think it's called. I'm sure they'd have a garrison of the national police there.''

He raised his brows. Apparently she'd done some homework on San Tomás. ''There's a man in the village where we're headed who can be trusted to get you back to the capital.'' Which was where she should have stayed. The local government made great efforts to keep the beaches safe for tourists from the cruise ships. ''Going south is out. Ruiz will have his troops watching the road.'' He shouldered his backpack.

She frowned. ''Who's Ruiz?''

''The man who sent soldiers to kidnap you. Let's go.''

''Wait a minute.'' She laid her hand on his arm. It was a small hand, surprisingly warm, with rounded fingernails that had been neatly manicured before she soaked them in a lake while hiding from guerrillas. Now the pretty pink polish was chipped. ''Who are you? I mean, I saw you on the bus, but we weren't introduced.''

''John,'' he said. It was as good a name as any, and the man he was taking her to thought of him as ''John.''

''John. I am *very* glad to meet you.'' She smiled, and her fingers tightened in a friendly squeeze. ''I'm Jane.''

Heat, quick and compelling, dazzled his system for one crazy moment.

''Thank you for—''

''Come on.'' He pulled away from her, looking for a game trail to take them deeper into the forest.

She scrambled after him, making every bit as much noise as he'd expected she would. ''What about west? Why aren't we going west instead of heading into the hills?''

''Go west if you want to. I'm going east.'' The strength of his reaction to her disturbed him. He was familiar with the effects of danger—the heightened senses, the rush of adrenaline, the occasional swift slide from sensory stimulation into arousal. But he'd never reacted this fast, this hard, before.

She'd only squeezed his arm, for heaven's sake. One simple squeeze, and his body had gone on full alert.

He didn't just want to kiss the woman now. He wanted to lay her down on the spongy floor of the forest, push up her dress, pull down her panties and push inside her. He wanted to ride her until they both screamed.

She followed without speaking. He'd almost hoped she'd turn around and head west—where, as she'd said, a town with a large garrison of the national police waited to welcome her back to what passed for civilization. Of course, Ruiz's men would almost certainly pick her up before she'd gone a mile.

They traveled in silence with him in the lead, moving slowly but steadily upward. The trails he took twisted and branched. He used the compass from his backpack to keep them heading in the right general direction, and by late afternoon they were deep in the rain forest and several hundred feet higher. The light here was shadowy and green, filtered by the leafy canopy overhead. Vague scurryings in the brush spoke of tiny lives being lived all around them, lives that had nothing to do with them. The man who called himself John was comforted by the indifference of his surroundings. Bit by bit, as they pressed farther into a world that cared not at all for their exalted status as humans, he relaxed back into his usual detachment.

It was just as well this was his last job. He'd known it was time to get out. Ever since Jack's death he had known, but his reactions today were so far out of line he had to wonder if he should have agreed to take this job, even as a favor. He owed Patrick a great deal, but messing up this job wouldn't repay him.

He heard a muffled squeak and turned. She was brushing frantically at something on her arm, a spider or some other small, multi-legged creature. "Did it bite you?" Concern hit him with a quick, unexpected punch. Few of the creepie-crawlies on the island were dangerous, but—

"No," she said. "Its wiggly little *legs* got on me." She looked as if she thought she'd been poisoned.

"You saved the other one," he pointed out. "In the lake. The beetle."

"It was going to drown." She rubbed her arm as if she hoped to wipe the insect germs off. "I couldn't just let it drown after... Well, the bug thought my arm was safe, and by holding still, I was sort of deceiving it. When it fell into the water, I felt responsible."

He looked at her, disbelieving. She'd felt responsible for a beetle? "Come on. I see a stump up ahead where you can sit. We need to get dry socks on."

"Why?" She limped after him. "Our shoes will still be wet."

"Jungle rot." He stopped by the stump to unzip his backpack. "One of the first rules in climate and terrain like this is to keep your feet dry." He handed her a pair of socks.

She shuddered and sat down.

He changed his own socks without sitting, balancing first on one leg, then the other, checking each foot for any small cuts or blisters. Open wounds in the tropics could be dangerous. When he had both shoes back on he looked at her and frowned. She was taking too long. She'd only done one foot. Her other foot was propped on her knee, her dress gathered up to her knees to droop in concealing folds between her parted legs. She was pulling the wet sock off slowly.

The sock had a wide, lacy border. It also had a red stain. "You're bleeding."

She eased the sock the rest of the way off. "Brilliant observation. Wet shoes and socks can rub blisters, you know."

He tightened his lips. "Leaving an open, untreated wound on the foot in a tropical zone is just begging for infection, fungus—" He shook his head, disgusted, as he unzipped the backpack. "What about your other foot?"

"It's fine."

He thought about the fact that she'd just kept going, without complaint, when her blister must have hurt like hell. "Take your shoe off." He got out the ointment and gauze. "I want to check both feet."

She had an odd expression on her face. "It's like my mother's purse."

"What?"

"Your backpack. It's like my mother's purse. She carries a tote the size of Manhattan, and it's got *everything* in it. Having you got a sewing kit in there?" she asked, interested.

As a matter of fact, he did. Among other things. He knelt in front of her and grabbed her foot.

"Hey!"

"Hold still." She had small feet, with pearly pink toenails. He couldn't keep from smiling when he saw those toenails. What was the point of painting them when she wasn't wearing sandals? He looked at the blister on her heel that had burst and bled into her sock. "Why didn't you tell me you were hurting?"

"Why? We couldn't have stopped any earlier, anyway, could we?"

"I need to know your limitations to plan properly." There was a topical anaesthetic in the ointment, and he would pad the area with gauze. That, and the dry socks, should make her more comfortable, but he wouldn't be able to keep her from hurting entirely. He frowned. Absently, he stroked his thumb along the bottom of her foot. It flexed in a quick, involuntary movement. "Are you ticklish?"

"N-no." Her eyes were dark when they met his. "I mean, yes."

He saw the heat in her eyes, heard the uncertain longing in her voice. His hand tightened on her foot as his body tightened elsewhere. Apparently he wasn't the only one coming down with jungle fever.

His gaze drifted away from her foot. Her dress was still damp. It molded nicely to the firm swells of her breasts, but he couldn't see her nipples anymore. Not quite. If he were to lean forward, though, and take one in his mouth…

No, he told himself. Not now. The time and the place were wrong. But it was harder than it should have been to look away, take the cap off the ointment, and tend to the part of her body that needed it most. And when he'd finished treating her blister, he stroked the sole of her foot again—one long, seemingly casual stroke of his thumb—and watched her foot quiver. No, he thought again, angry with her for responding so quickly and easily. He wouldn't take her. It wasn't safe; not here and now.

But maybe it would be. Later.

Jane caught glimpses of the sun whenever the forest canopy thinned. It was on its way down now, though they still had some daylight left. The man who'd rescued her kept moving tirelessly while she watched, and followed.

Observing him was altogether too pleasant. He was lithe and muscular and graceful, and Jane's body couldn't seem to understand that he wasn't at all what she wanted, no matter how firmly she spoke to it. She didn't understand it. Her dress was filthy and wrinkled; her feet hurt with every step; she was tired and lost, and mystified by her body's reactions. After twenty-nine years of reasonable behavior, it seemed determined to embarrass her with outrageous demands.

She felt as if she'd started the day in Kansas and ended up in Oz. Only instead of ruby slippers, all she had to get her home were her filthy tennis shoes, and instead of a friendly Scarecrow or Tin Man, her companion was a cold-eyed liar who made her body burn.

So his name was John, was it?

After noticing the way he'd stared at her breasts, she'd kept her distance from him, not asking questions, though she was nearly bursting with them. Except her foolish body wasn't listening to her sensible brain.

Maybe, she thought as they started up yet another a hill,

this sudden attack of lust was part of the price she had to pay for her foolishness. A solitary, impromptu vacation had seemed like such a small adventure, though. Most of the time, Jane felt mildly foolish about her other name—the one her father had given her—but she'd wanted just once to see if she could live up to it. A woman whose middle name was Desirée ought to be able to handle all sorts of risks.

Which proved how little she deserved such an exotic name, she thought glumly. She would much rather have been helping Frances Ann get her garden ready the way she'd planned to do before Ed had waved that cruise ticket under her nose. Instead, she was on the run with a man who might be a spy. Or a criminal.

At least her inconvenient lust took her mind off the way her feet hurt. "How much farther do you suppose this village is?"

"Hard to say, when we haven't been traveling in a straight line."

No, they hadn't, had they? He'd gone out of his way to avoid that, and she wondered why. Jane added that to the mental list she was keeping of questions to ask at a better time, when she wasn't out of breath and her reluctant rescuer seemed a little friendlier. But what if things didn't get better? she asked herself suddenly, pausing to catch her breath. What if things stayed messed up and scary, and the man in front of her stayed silent and scary?

Damn. Jane bit her lip. He was heading downhill, annoyingly tireless. She skidded after him—and spoke up. "So why *aren't* we traveling in a straight line? Why didn't we take that little dirt road we passed a while back?"

"It was going in the wrong direction."

That sounded good, and yet… Jane consulted her mental list as she made her way unsteadily downhill after him.

His pants were dry now. They should have been too baggy to be sexy, but watching him move did funny things to her breathing. He was as lithe as a dancer, but it was a deadly sort of grace—one that spoke of both survival and danger.

Moves like an athlete or a martial-arts expert, she added to her mental list.

That list kept growing. He had known about General Ruiz. He'd done something violent and serious to the two soldiers when he rescued her. He didn't like roads, or even well-traveled footpaths. He knew about this village that was, apparently, the only place he considered safe; and that, in itself, didn't make sense.

"Why is this village the only safe spot for us to go?" she asked. "Why didn't we go west?"

He didn't bother to look back. "Generalissimo Ruiz has his camp set up a few miles west of the village where our bus stopped. I doubt that it needed repairs, by the way. The driver had probably been bribed to deliver the *norteamericanos* to the village. Ruiz has done this before, grabbing any foreigners who wander near what he considers his territory. He's after ransom."

"But I don't have any money!"

He shrugged. "If he couldn't get money from your family, he'd try to get it from his government, which can't afford to be embarrassed by his little tricks. The cruise ships will stop docking here if they start losing tourists to Ruiz's plans for redistributing the wealth."

They'd reached the bottom of the gully, where a trickle of water pretended to be a stream. He headed south along the would-be streambed.

Jane scrambled after him. He had to be either a spy or a criminal, didn't he? Who else would know the kinds of things he did? She shuddered at the possibility that she might be at the mercy of someone who sold drugs or guns—a man with no morals and no conscience.

But would a man like that have saved her? She couldn't believe it.

Of course, this whole situation veered between the incredible and the unbelievable. Here we are, she thought, John and Jane, tramping through the jungle, pursued by rebel guerrillas.... She frowned. "What did you say your name was?"

"John."

"Now that's original. John Doe, maybe?"

He turned around. The gleam in his eyes might have been amusement. Or a warning. "I should remember that naïveté isn't the same as stupidity. Let's make it Smith."

Her heart beat faster. "What a coincidence. My name's Smith, too."

His mouth thinned. "Sure, it is. Look, you don't need to know who I am. Just do what I tell you, and don't ask questions."

Shutting up sounded like a good idea, except now that she'd gotten started, she couldn't seem to stop. "I don't see what difference it makes. You're just going to lie about the answers anyway."

"The less you think you know, the better. There are people who wouldn't let you leave the country if they suspected you knew me." He paused. "Pay attention, Jane. This is what really happened. You were frightened by the gunfire and ran. You got lost, but kept going because you didn't know what else to do. You don't know how you wound up near a village where a nice man found you, and offered to escort you to the capital. You never saw me after the bus stopped for repairs."

She bit her lip. "Are you a spy?"

For a second his face went blank. When he smiled, it looked as graceful and intentional as everything else he did. "Sure. I'm a spy, Jane. Just like James Bond and all the other good guys."

She was pretty certain he was nothing like James Bond, maybe nothing like any of the good guys. But he *had* rescued her. Surely that meant he had a conscience.

"So worried," he murmured, his gaze sliding down from

her face. "If you're frightened of me, why do you stay with me?"

He was looking at her again. At her breasts. And his eyes weren't cold now, not at all. As for her traitorous body... She resisted the urge to cross her arms in front of her and hide its reaction.

He came toward her. "Jane—"

She took one quick step back so she wouldn't throw herself up against him—and tripped, landing hard on her bottom.

Now his smile was genuine—and amused, damn him. "I was just going to ask what your real last name is."

"Smith," she muttered, and stood with far less grace than he used to just stand there and breathe. She rubbed her sore bottom.

"I'm glad you have a sense of humor, Jane, but I need your real name."

"Well, John *Smith*, we don't always get what we want, do we? But in this case you did. My real name is Smith. Jane Smith. From Atherton, Kansas."

"Your parents actually named you Jane Smith?" He grinned.

Oh, Lord, when he grinned like that he became yet another person—this one, lively and compelling. "It's my curse," she said weakly. It wasn't fair that all his personas were so blasted sexy. "I always have to show ID. People don't believe anyone is really named Jane Smith."

He held out his hand. "In any case, I'm glad to meet you, Jane Smith of Atherton, Kansas."

She hesitated only a second before accepting his outstretched hand. They shook. "And I'm delighted to meet you, John Smith of...wherever."

"Never-Never Land, do you think? Or maybe Oz."

Startled by how he'd echoed her earlier thoughts, she laughed.

"Ah, Jane," he said, and closed his other hand over hers.

The light in his eyes wasn't amusement now. "You're not in Kansas anymore, are you?"

It was the oddest feeling, having her hand trapped between both of his that way. Odd, and...stimulating. Her pulse thrummed in her throat. She swallowed. "No. This definitely isn't Kansas."

He stood there without speaking. His fingers played with hers, stroking one, then another, but she had the impression he wasn't paying attention to what his hands did. She was, though. His casual claiming of her hand sent tingles zipping through her system like the air-drawn streamers trailed by a Fourth of July sparkler. But he seemed entirely focused on her face.

On *her*.

It was the most erotic thing she'd ever experienced. Her lips parted and her breathing grew shallow, because he *wanted* her. It wasn't fair. Men seldom noticed her. Certainly she'd never expected this frightening man, this cold-eyed liar of a man, to notice her. Her fantasies should have stayed safe, private....

He smiled a quiet, knowing smile, as if he'd seen right inside her head to where those fantasies were lodged; as if he knew exactly what they were—and intended to do something about them. Then he blinked. His eyes lost their focus, and he went still, like a cat just before it jumps on a mouse. His head lifted.

"What?" she whispered, looking around in alarm. "What is it?"

He dropped her hand and held his finger to his mouth as he had hours ago, signaling her to silence. They stood motionless, and she strained her ears for a long moment before she heard what he had heard—a voice.

No, several voices. Distant still, but coming this way along the streambed.

Three

There was nothing lover-like about the way he grabbed her hand this time. He dragged her back up the side of the gully with him, but he was confusingly arbitrary about how he moved, zigzagging all over the place. When he snatched her back from a bare patch of ground, she realized he was staying on the grassy patches so they wouldn't leave tracks.

That did nothing to quiet the frantic alarm signals her heart was pounding out.

They reached a thicket of tall grasses and weeds shadowed by the trees behind them. The voices were nearer—much nearer. He tugged her down with him, so that they lay flat on their stomachs. She felt giddy, her breath coming fast and shallow. He scooted forward, so she did, too, and she saw why he'd chosen this spot. Here, the shadows of the trees fell over them, dense and concealing. They could peer through the cover offered by the weeds, but no one below would be able to see them—not as long as they were still.

Jane knew she could hold still. She'd proved that much in

the lake. This should be easier. She had dry ground beneath her, and his warm body beside her. Unfortunately, his body was every bit as distracting as the monster bug had been—but in a different way.

She stared down at the little trickle of a stream, her muscles tight with fear and the need for stillness. Two men came into view. They wore uniforms, familiar uniforms that made Jane go limp with relief. These were *federales,* members of the semimilitary national police. The cops, she thought, giddy with regained safety. The good guys. She started to turn to John, to tell him they were safe, but her head never finished the motion.

His hand clamped over her mouth. Again. She jolted, then glared at him out of the corner of her eye.

He brought his mouth next to her ear, as he had before. "Shh. Look before you leap, Jane. An isolated squad of soldiers may not be a safe escort for a woman alone," he breathed. Slowly he removed his hand from her mouth.

Below them, three more of the national police moved into view. She frowned, confused, and watched. The men in the little gully weren't a reassuring sight. They were dirty and unshaven and they slouched along, weapons at the ready, joking with each other or snarling complaints. They didn't act very military. One of them said something that made her think they were looking for something.

Or someone.

No one would have mounted a search for her—not this quickly. She glanced at the man beside her. They lay so close together on the ground that she could smell him. The faint, welcoming note of human warmth was almost lost in the earthy odor of the humus covering the forest floor beneath them. Silently she mouthed, "Who are they looking for?"

His gaze met hers. His lips smiled, but those vastly blue eyes of his were cold. He brought his mouth close again in that disconcerting simulation of a lover's approach, so that his voice was a puff of barely heard words on her skin. "Me.

So if you're tired of my company, sweet Jane, all you have to do is attract their attention.''

The authorities were after him? She jerked—not much; just one quick, involuntary motion away from a man who might be the criminal she didn't believe him to be.

A pebble rolled down the hill.

She froze in horror.

At first she thought it would be all right. Then one of the men said something, pointing in their direction. A couple of them stopped and peered upward. One chided the others for being jumpy, and the first man defended himself angrily. A fourth man—maybe he was a sergeant or an officer; he had a cleaner uniform—came back to see what the argument was about.

The man beside her stiffened. She turned her head slowly.

He wasn't looking at her. Or at the *federales*. A bead of sweat trickled slowly down his temple as he stared at his left hand, the one farthest from her.

A snake slithered slowly across his outspread hand.

It paused, a pretty creature a little more than a foot long, the green, scaly body crossed by narrow white bands. It looked like a chubby green rope. Jane tried telling herself that short, chubby snakes weren't as scary as long, sleek ones, but fear sucked her brain empty, and the thought wouldn't stick.

The snake raised its flat, lance-shaped head, opened its mouth and tasted the air with rapid flicks of its tongue.

Only inches separated the snake's mouth from John's face.

Panic crawled over her like a swarm of ants. She wanted to move—wanted it with a twitchy physical craving she'd never known before—but if she moved, if she even breathed too hard, the snake might bite John. She had managed to stay still with that bug on her. She could do this. She *had* to, or it would bite him and he would die. Right there beside her he would die, and it would be all her fault.

She told herself desperately that most snakes weren't venomous. John was holding very, very still, so maybe he didn't know this. She wasn't sure he was even breathing.

The snake lowered its head and moved forward. Over John's hand. Across the ground. And straight toward Jane's hand.

She thought she'd faint.

It sampled the air near her clenched fist. When had she closed her fingers up tight like that? Now she couldn't relax them. She thought furiously "vegetable" thoughts at the snake: I am a green, leafy plant. I am warm from the sun, not from blood. You can't eat me. I am a green, leafy plant....

The snake's tongue flicked over her skin. She stopped breathing. Her vision dimmed.

But she didn't move.

The snake turned away from her hand and slithered casually on into the thicket.

She watched as it slid through the grass, heading slowly downhill. Her chest hurt. She remembered to breathe, which helped. She wondered if the snake would go all the way down to the gully and bite one of the soldiers.

The second the snake vanished from sight, she felt a hand on hers.

This time, she didn't jump. She turned her head.

John nodded once. *What is that supposed to mean?* she wondered hysterically. *Hello? How are you today? Seen any good snakes lately?* Then he started inching backward on his stomach. Alarmed, she glanced down and saw that while they'd been occupied—literally—by the snake, the soldiers had moved along the gully and out of sight.

She was more than ready to follow her rescuer's lead this time.

They inched backward until they could stand. As soon as she was on her feet he took her hand again.

They ran hand in hand down one of the trails, him ahead, her behind, and no doubt he was fully in control of himself and had sound, logical reasons for making such a speedy escape. Jane ran because it felt so damned good to run. She didn't want to stop. She didn't want to see another bug or soldier or slithery green snake ever again—or any part of a forest, either. But the forest was all around them, and no matter how hard they ran, she couldn't get away from it.

He slowed and stopped, pulling her off the trail with him into a small, sun-dappled spot, a patch of ground where some mystery of the soil had caused the trees and underbrush to thin. There was enough sunlight for a bit of grass to spread itself out. Scraps of blue showed through overhead, laced by the leaves of the few branches that arced above the pocket-size clearing.

"I'm not tired," Jane said, gasping for breath and clutching her side. "I can keep going."

"Hey." He turned her to face him. "It's all right. We're far enough away from them now." He took her other hand in his, too, and smiled at her.

"I—I—" She couldn't catch her breath. He wasn't winded, damn him, and his ponytail was still neat. "I hate snakes!" she exclaimed. "I hate snakes, I really do. I just hate them, but I couldn't move. At first it would have bit you and then it would have bit me, but I—I—" Her breath caught in a hiccup that was perilously close to a sob.

"I know," he said, and pulled her up against him and put his arms around her. "You hate snakes."

He was warm and solid and she clutched at him, delirious from lack of oxygen. "I know you're not laughing at me," she told him. "Because if you were, I'd have to kill you, and I don't have my breath back yet."

"I'm not laughing," he assured her, and his hand stroked down her back. "You did good back there. Real good. I thought I was dead. I would have been, if you'd startled the snake. You saved my life by keeping your head."

She had rescued *him?* The thought made her even more dizzy. "Then it was poisonous? I thought maybe you were just scared of snakes, too."

"I think it was a fer-de-lance. They're rare, and I've never seen one in person before, so I could be wrong. It could have been another of the bothrops—that's a genus of pit viper found in Central and South America."

She pulled away suspiciously. "You know an awful lot about snakes. Are you some kind of—of herpetologist or something?"

"I thought we'd agreed that I was a spy." His expression was solemn, but his eyes were bright with mirth.

"You *are* laughing at me."

"You sounded so horrified," he said apologetically.

"Well, spying I could understand, but why anyone would want to spend their life studying *snakes*—"

He chuckled.

She blinked and managed to be offended for one whole second before her own absurdity tricked her into giggling. "I r-really don't like snakes," she said between giggles, and this struck her as so exquisitely funny that she went off into peals of laughter—at herself, at him, at the whole silly show of life, because she was so very glad she was still a part of it.

He didn't laugh. His eyes changed, darkening, but that was the only notice she had. It wasn't enough of a warning, not when she was laughing so hard her vision was blurred by tears.

When his mouth closed over hers, her laughter stopped.

His lips were smooth and firm and beguiling, and she smelled him—oh, she breathed him right in, and he went to her head like wine. She made one sound of protest, but he ignored that, just as he ignored the hand she put on his chest to hold him back. He simply moved her hand out of his way while his other hand slipped to her bottom and scooped her up against him.

It was too much, too fast. She'd lurched from terror to flight, skidded from flight into laughter, and now she was being ruthlessly kissed by a man who made her knees silly and her soul shiver. In a day already ripped loose from everything Jane knew about herself and her world, the sudden surge of passion caught her and flung her into a mad riptide she had no way of resisting.

When he pushed his thigh between her legs and pressed up, she heard herself moan. And it *was* her. She was the one making those soft, urgent sounds. She had to stop this, stop him—only he pressed up again with his thigh, and his tongue wet her lips while his hands, both hands now, kneaded her bottom, lifting her, then pressing her down on the leg she straddled. He taught her to ride him, taught her a slow, rolling rhythm that carried her mind the rest of the way out to sea, and left her body in charge.

And her body knew what it wanted.

He pulled her down with him. The forest floor was damp and spongy, and the moist, fecund odor was almost as intoxicating as the way he smelled when she pressed her face to his neck.

He didn't unfasten her clothing. He ran his hands over her as if there was no part of her he didn't need to feel, to know. Her knee, her breast, her shoulder. The soft swell of her belly. But he didn't take her clothes off, which gave her a spurious sense of safety.

Then his mouth left hers and closed over the tip of her breast. Right through her dress and her bra he suckled her, and no one had ever done that to her. She hadn't even known people *did* that—not with their clothes on—and she was almost shocked back into conscious thought. Almost. But by then he had her dress and her bra wet from his mouth, and he did things with his tongue and his teeth that rasped the dampened material against her sensitive nipple, and she moaned instead, and clutched at his shoulders.

His mouth moved to her other breast, and that was good, too; that was what she wanted. He sucked. She felt his hand on her leg, and it was drawing her skirt up, and that felt good, too—the warmth of his palm on her thigh, on her—

She yelped when he pressed his palm against her *there,* right between her legs. He slid a finger beneath the elastic of her panties and touched her even more intimately, and she moaned again, and this time she shocked herself, because her hips lifted pleadingly.

"I—I—" she stammered. "I don't—ah—"

He licked her nipple. His finger slid inside her feminine folds and rubbed her lightly. She made a sound she'd never made before, and her hips turned wanton again, making that greedy pushing-at-him movement. But she held on to the thin thread of consciousness and gripped his shoulders hard, willing him to look at her.

He raised his head. His mouth was wet and his eyes gleamed with hunger, and his finger was still moving, stirring her unbearably. He looked so entirely delicious she knew this was her last chance. "I don't do this sort of thing!" she gasped.

"But I do, Jane," he said gently, and he moved his hand, stretching the elastic of her panties so that his finger went up inside her. "I do."

And he did, too. First he kissed her again. And he tasted like danger, but he also felt like safety and home—solid and strong and eager for her, so eager. Maybe she could have fought her own hunger, the need that had grown in her all day. She couldn't resist his.

He wasn't cold now. Now he burned just as she did. Now he needed her.

And when he pulled her panties down and shifted between her legs, she helped him. He gripped her hips in his hands and guided himself inside, and the sensation was so rich and huge it almost sent her over the top right then.

Her eyes closed. She slipped her hands inside his loosened shirt, and delighted in his skin. "John," she gasped. "John."

He didn't move. He was fully, firmly inside her, but he wasn't *doing* anything. Jane wasn't exactly a woman of the world, but she knew what was supposed to be happening now, and it wasn't.

She opened her eyes and looked up at him.

His eyes were full of all sorts of blue—the restless blues of oceans and ghosts and sorrow, and the hot blue at the heart of a flame. "My name isn't John," he said softly. Then, at last, he began to move.

She was warm and limp beneath him. Instinct or some last gasp of reason had kept him braced on his elbows so that now, as he slowly seeped back into himself after the sensory explosion of climax, his upper body, at least, wasn't crushing her.

Unlike her, he was still fully dressed. But he felt naked. Trapped and naked and exposed.

Fear was a swell he rode, a great, ocean-deep wave too vast and familiar for panic. Reason rode the wave with him— a slim craft he clung to. But reason told him he had just made himself into a fool. Fools died quickly in his business. And sometimes they caused other people to lose their lives, too.

He looked at the woman beneath him. Her eyes were closed. A half smile curved her lips. Sweat dampened her face and shoulders, making her glow. The little chain she wore around her neck hung crooked now. The locket dangled in the dust beside her.

Ah, Jane.

He pushed off her. "Get up." Grimly he put himself to rights and zipped his pants.

She blinked up at him, obviously confused, a trickle of hurt altering the curve of her mouth. He had to force his voice to soften, but it took no effort at all to reach out one more time and cup her cheek; her skin was so soft. "I'm sorry," he said more gently. "I've endangered both of us. We have to get out of here, quickly."

His shirt hung outside his pants. It was partly unbuttoned.

He remembered her hands—such warm, avid hands—struggling to undo a few buttons so she could stroke his chest.

She did sit up, but then just sat there, looking bewildered. The skirt of her dress slipped from her waist to puddle in her lap. Her bodice was still damp over one nipple. "You didn't put us in danger," she said. "There's no one around."

She didn't understand. He'd forgotten everything but the need to bury himself in her. That went beyond danger to sheer foolhardiness. How could he have lost control so completely?

He'd been doing all right until she'd laughed.

He tightened his lips. "The *federales* we saw were looking for me. They intend to shoot me, Jane, not take me prisoner."

"But *why?*"

He hesitated, but there was no reason not to tell her this much. "I have information some people don't want leaving the country, and those people have enough money to bribe any number of government officials. If you're with me when they find me, they'll kill you, too. I have to get you to the village so I can get the hell off this island." He didn't want to die on his last assignment. He didn't want to see this bright, plucky woman shot down because she was with him.

She bit her lip, her eyes wide with fear. Slowly, she stood. "Who are you?" she whispered. "*What* are you?"

He met her gaze, and wondered if the sadness he felt showed. "Who and what I am doesn't matter at all. You can forget me under the name 'John' as well as you could under another name."

"I'm not going to—"

"You will. You have to."

Three hours later, Jane sat on a cot in a rapidly-darkening room in a village whose name she still hadn't heard. Her host, a British expatriot, was in the parlor of the small but pleasant house, talking secrets with the man whose name wasn't John.

He had to leave her here, she knew. He couldn't stay and be found by the government troops quartering the area for him. She knew he had to leave and she knew she would never see him again, but she sat there and waited for him to at least come and say goodbye.

He never did.

Four

It was not yet dark, but the light was fading as dusk slowly replaced daylight. In an old frame house on a street lined with elms, a light came on in an upstairs window. Most people in town still referred to the old house as "the MacAllister place," though all but one of that family had died or moved away years ago. The one remaining MacAllister, Frances Ann, lived downstairs with her cats, her needlepoint and her family albums.

Jane lived upstairs.

She flipped on the light switch in her kitchen and hurried to the pantry. She pushed aside the gingersnaps, the rice and two boxes of breakfast cereal, muttering under her breath. She was due at the meeting of the Atherton Combined Charities in fifteen minutes. As secretary for the community-wide fund-raising project, she absolutely had to be there. But she was not leaving without her crackers.

She probably wouldn't be late, she told herself as she switched her search to the second shelf. Even if she had to stop and buy more crackers, she had time. She could get from anywhere in Atherton to anywhere else in fifteen minutes, usually with time to spare. But she didn't want to get into her car without crackers. Although she seemed to be over the stomach bug that had afflicted her off and on for the past two weeks, she wasn't taking any chances. The nausea might come back when she started driving.

Ah. She straightened as her hands touched a cellophane-wrapped package. Success.

Jane grabbed her purse, shrugged it onto her shoulder and flipped on her porch light. It would be dark by the time she came home. She stepped out onto the landing and was just pulling her front door closed when the phone rang. She froze.

Her hand went to her chest. She could barely feel the lump her locket made beneath the wool of her favorite pink sweater. Her fingers pressed against that tiny lump. Don't be silly, she scolded herself. It was probably her mother, calling to check on her. Marilee Smith's normal fretfulness had escalated to nearly unbearable levels since Jane had returned from the island.

She really ought to go back inside and reassure her mother, but—

The phone rang again.

But what if it was *him?*

It wasn't, of course. She knew that. He'd had three weeks to call if he were going to. He hadn't. And why should he? What had happened between them had meant nothing to him, obviously. He hadn't bothered to say goodbye.

She didn't even know if he was still alive.

No, whoever was calling now, it certainly wasn't the man who'd been her lover for fifteen life-changing minutes. And dammit, she wasn't going to do this to herself anymore. She'd stopped crying, hadn't she?

The tears that had come at odd, unpredictable moments for the first week after she'd arrived home had embarrassed her as much as they had worried her mother. Trauma could have odd effects on a person, but she was done with that. She had nothing to cry about. Nor did she intend to spend any more nights staring at her ceiling with her mind racing like a hamster running itself crazy on its wheel. She would never know if her mysterious rescuer had lived to leave the island or not, and staying awake worrying about him was as pointless as it was pathetic.

But Jane couldn't silence the frantic little voice inside that said that this time the call *might* be from him. What if it was?

The phone rang again.

She rubbed the small lump that her locket made. *Papa,* she thought wistfully, *did you ever wonder if some of the chances you took might not have been worth what you risked? Or am I just a coward?* Probably she was a coward. Hadn't she proved how poor she was at coping with danger? Look at what she'd done—made passionate love with a man whose name she didn't know. Passionate, unprotected love.

Slowly, Jane pulled the door closed behind her. This wasn't the first call she had refused to answer since she'd gotten home—just in case.

The wind was picking up. It ruffled her hair as she stood on the landing looking down at her reliable old Toyota. She took a steadying breath and promised herself that tomorrow she would buy a Caller ID machine so she wouldn't freak out every time her phone rang.

She pulled a cracker from the package she carried and nibbled on it as she started down the steps.

Samuel Charmaneaux pulled off into the rest area at the top of a low hill. He sat in the three-year-old black Jeep Cherokee he'd bought last week, though the registration showed he'd bought it new. The name on that registration matched the one on his driver's license, birth certificate and all the other papers that made a person real in today's world.

He turned off the stereo and rolled down the window, wanting to listen to the wind that blew here. To taste it.

Samuel had been planning this for months. Oh, not all of it. He'd had to wait on circumstances to supply some details. Certainly the particular detail that had brought him nearly fifteen hundred miles across the country hadn't been part of his original plan, but Samuel's plans were always fluid. Objectives were the fixed points in his universe, and he was very good at achieving his objectives.

Good, but not perfect. His eyes darkened as he remembered the sound of Jack choking on his own blood as he'd fought for breath. Samuel had been far less than perfect that day. He didn't exactly blame himself for his friend's death, but he accepted the burden of it, knowing he'd been part of the events that had led to it. With that acceptance had come a certainty: he could no longer be part of the world he'd lived in for the past ten years.

At first, he hadn't known what he would do instead. He still wasn't sure, but he knew what his new objective was. Samuel wanted to be part of the world that other people knew. The ordinary world.

It wasn't going to be easy. The official records of his new identity would hold up under much stronger scrutiny than he should ever receive, but he wasn't as sure of himself as he was of his papers. He was used to living under other names, living bits and pieces of borrowed lives, but this was different. This time it would be for the rest of his life. And for the first time in years, "the rest of his life" meant more than just the next job.

Having a future was going to take some getting used to.

To the west, the sun still shone at the rim of the world, but twilight was seeping up from its eastern edge, blurring the outlines of things. Samuel looked down at the small town of Atherton, where lights were blinking on in houses as dusk drew near.

He hadn't expected hills.

Admittedly, these hills weren't much. Compared to their grander cousins in other parts of the world, such as the tumbled hills of Provence or the worn heights crowding the ancient city of Dharmsala, these were barely lumps. But the fact that he'd had expectations that weren't grounded in experience or research bothered him. He was a thorough man. He'd gotten a background check on the town as well as the woman, yet apparently he'd allowed his thinking to be colored by ideas formed about Kansas when he was very young. He'd expected pancake-flat land—not this green, gently rolling country laced with streams.

He shook his head, disgusted. Had he expected to meet a young girl and her little dog, Toto, too?

It had been a long drive, and Samuel's left palm ached in spite of the care he'd taken with it. He rested his hand on his thigh and began rhythmically opening and closing the hand. The exercise made it hurt more, of course, but the pain was easy enough to ignore. What he couldn't ignore was the impairment. His fingers still wouldn't close tightly.

It's been less than two weeks since the surgery, he reminded himself. He refused to believe he wouldn't regain any more function than this.

Thunder rumbled off to the west. It was early April, and spring meant storms in this part of the world. His gaze returned to the town at the foot of the hill, and he thought about the future and his plans.

Jane Smith was down there. Jane *Desirée* Smith, he thought, smiling as he remembered the report he'd read, which had given her full name. Her middle name suited her. On the surface, she was wonderfully ordinary, but there were surprises inside. He thought about pretty Jane of the innocent eyes and delicious body, practical Jane who had climaxed with such amazement. Jane, who hated snakes and rescued beetles and kept walking without complaint while her feet bled into her lacy socks.

What was she doing right now? Was she with her family? Was she laughing or sad or worried?

Had she thought about him today?

Determination clenched inside him. She would think of him soon. And soon, he would have an answer to the question that would determine the shape of his future.

The sudden, hot pain startled him. He looked at his hands. He was holding the steering wheel tightly; his knuckles were white. The left hand hurt fiercely, as if struggling to obey, but would not close fully.

He didn't even remember gripping the wheel.

Shaken, he relaxed his grip. It was definitely time to retire, if his emotions could control him that way. He took one last, lingering look at the town below. Long habit had him evaluating it in tactical terms, matching what he saw to the map he'd studied earlier, but the feeling that welled up in him as he put the Cherokee into gear had little to do with tactics.

He didn't have a name for what he felt. The gentle tugging deep inside was nothing he recognized. It didn't seem strong enough to disturb his control, however, so he ignored it as he had ignored the pain, and pulled away from the rest stop.

It was no wonder the feeling was unfamiliar. The man who was now named Samuel had never come home before.

"Jane!"

"Hmm? Oh." Jane realized she'd let her thoughts drift off. That had happened too often lately. Hastily she closed the notebook where she'd jotted down the minutes. "Sorry. I was thinking." Glancing around, she saw that she was the only one still seated in the conference room, though a number of people were milling around, chatting or making their way to the door. "Did you ask me something, Sandy?"

Sandy Clemmons was the local Red Cross director. She was a plump, pretty woman several years older than Jane whose calm temperament disproved the stereotypes about redheads. "Are you okay?"

"I'm fine." Jane pushed her chair back and stood.

"Are you sure? It's none of my business, but I can't help

noticing that you've acted different ever since you got back from that trip.''

"I said I'm fine." Jane grabbed her purse and her coat.

Sandy's eyebrows went up. "Heard that sort of comment a little too often, maybe?"

Jane's mouth twitched in reluctant humor. "Have you been talking to my mother? She wants me to consider therapy. And eat more vegetables." The suggestions were typical of Marilee Smith, who had also mentioned a CAT scan, earlier bedtimes and Saint-John's-wort as possible cures for whatever ailed her youngest child.

"Well, you did have a dreadful experience."

Everyone in town knew that Jane had nearly been taken prisoner by rebel soldiers. And that was all anyone knew, in spite of the determined efforts of several people, including her mother, to learn more. "It was scary, but it's over." Jane slipped her arms into her coat and assured herself she spoke nothing but the truth. "What was it you asked me while I was thinking?"

"I wondered if you were planning to drive into Kansas City for the workshops the regional Red Cross is co-sponsoring with the Federal Emergency Management Agency. This is the last time they'll be offered for quite a while, and I can't miss the opportunity. I wouldn't mind having someone to share the ride."

"Uh—no, I don't think so."

"I know you're interested in disaster relief. You've taken all sorts of first-aid courses and emergency-response courses."

"For all the good it does me." Jane smiled ruefully. "I still get sick at the sight of blood."

"But there are other ways to help than by bandaging people. These workshops are designed for the people who organize volunteers in an emergency situation."

Jane was startled by the idea that someone thought her

capable of that sort of thing. Before she could answer, someone else called her name.

"I'll talk with you about it later," Sandy said, giving Jane a friendly smile before she moved away

There wasn't anything more to discuss, but Jane didn't have a chance to say that. It probably wouldn't have mattered if she had, she thought gloomily. No one listened to her, anyway; they all wanted to talk to her, but no one listened.

Bob Burgoman and his wife caught her before she could escape from the conference room. Bob asked her opinion on U.S. relations with Central America as a not-so-subtle prelude to digging for dirt about what had happened to her on San Tomás. Jane fidgeted and tried to get away, but her hints about needing to get home were ignored.

Why did everyone feel entitled to her story, anyway?

Fortunately, Liza came swooping by. Liza was a five-foot-two-inch bulldozer with a smile to put a game-show host to shame. She turned that smile on the Burgomans, said she hoped they didn't mind but she had to talk to Jane for a minute. Then she dragged Jane willy-nilly out into the hall.

"How do you get away with that?" Jane asked as they started down the wide corridor. "If I acted that way, people would be offended."

"People expect me to be rude. They're used to it. Now, I want to know what you thought you could accomplish by avoiding me lately."

"I'm sick of being interrogated. And I'm sick of being some sort of sensation for everyone to marvel over."

"If you don't want to be a sensation, you shouldn't do sensational things." Liza's words weren't sympathetic, but the pat she gave Jane's arm was. "Now, I know some of what happened, but no more than everyone else does, which is a sorry state when I'm supposed to be your best friend." Liza frowned at her. "You were chased through a swamp—"

"It wasn't a swamp." Jane started down the carpeted stairs. The meeting had been held in the hushed dignity of the conference room on the second story of the Atherton National Bank because it was the only place large enough to accommodate everyone. Representatives from all of the area's charitable organizations and many of its businesses were involved in the charity drive that would kick off soon with the Charity Ball.

"Your mom said something about bugs and water, so I assumed there was a swamp in there someplace."

"I think the committee needs to focus more on the corporate donors this year, don't you?"

Liza, normally a tireless advocate for the women's shelter where she volunteered, ignored that feeble attempt to change the subject. "You escaped from the swamp—or whatever—into the jungle. Soldiers with guns were looking for you." She sighed. "Nothing like that has ever happened to me."

"Get that envious note out of your voice. You can't possibly want to be chased by men with guns."

"Oh, I don't know. It sounds exciting. There you were, alone in the jungle—"

"I wasn't alone." Immediately she regretted having said that. "There were monkeys and—and birds. And a snake." And lions and tigers and bears, oh my. She dug into her purse and pulled out what was left of her crackers.

"You know what I mean." They'd reached the foot of the stairs. Liza, her chin tucked down in a manner that gave her an unfortunate resemblance to a bulldog, stopped to look sternly at Jane. "There is something you're not telling me about your little island adventure."

"I haven't told you anything about it."

"You acted like this when Doug dumped you—all mopey and quiet."

"Doug didn't 'dump' me. We mutually agreed to break our engagement." Jane started for the front door. She wanted to be alone. Normally she loved being around people, but not lately. If only everyone wouldn't keep talking and talking about the island—what had happened there, or what they thought had happened, or what hadn't happened but might have.... Jane sighed as she reached the double doors. She shoved one open and stepped outside.

A lot of the committee members hadn't yet left, in spite of the chilly weather. They stood around chatting, bunched up together beneath the nearest light pole.

"You always get like this when you're upset," her friend the bulldog said. "Like when your father died. You try to pull your head into your shell like a turtle. I'm not trying to be a pest, believe it or not. I'm worried about you."

"Good grief, Liza, you're exaggerating things all out of proportion. This is nothing like when Papa died." She didn't know that her rescuer had died, Jane reminded herself as she huddled into her coat. It was colder than it had any right to be, with spring just around the corner. And she was not going to think about hot, steamy forests.

"So maybe no one died, but you're acting as if—"

"Jane!" It was Cece Leithmason, former cheerleader and bane of Jane's high-school years. She bounced over and grabbed Jane's hands. "Oh, Jane, you sly thing—why didn't you tell us?"

Jane blinked and tried to get her hands back. "Tell you what?"

"About *him!* Oh, I suppose you wanted to surprise us, but you are too bad!" Cecilia dropped Jane's hands so she could wag a finger in her face. "We found you out!"

There was something wrong with Jane's breathing. Her chest was moving, but she didn't seem to be getting enough air. "I—I don't know what you mean."

A man stepped out of the crowd clustered beneath the light pole. He wore an expensive-looking dark trench coat with tailored black slacks. His hair was pulled back in a neat ponytail, revealing a face both beautiful and alien, a face that didn't belong in quiet little Atherton. In the harsh glow of the streetlamp, his eyes didn't look the brilliant blue she remembered; they looked dark and secretive.

He was alive. He'd made it off the island and he was *here*. And he had those glasses on. Those damned, lying, gold-rimmed glasses.

Jane didn't know if she was going to scream or faint.

When he smiled and came toward her, she stopped being able to hear the people around her. He stopped in front of her. "Sweetheart," he said in a voice she'd dreamed of at night and done her best to forget the next morning. "I know you weren't expecting me. Surprised?" He reached for her.

Too numb with disbelief to speak, she put up her hands to ward him off.

He caught them in his. "Your friends have been making me welcome while I waited for you." He pulled her hands against his chest, and, off-balance, she followed, landing up against him.

The feelings when their bodies touched were the same— dizzying, splendid. She couldn't stand it.

"Now it's your turn to welcome me." He bent his head.

If he tried to kiss her, she would bite him. Jane prepared to defend herself, but his mouth brushed her temple, not her lips. Frantically she told herself that she did *not* feel anything when he did that—not a thing. Certainly no sweet sizzle that almost drowned out the sound of his low chuckle. "Behave yourself." He spoke in the barely-there voice he'd used when they were hiding from the *federales*.

"Let go of me or I'll—I'll have you arrested!" she whispered.

"No, I think you'll take me home with you instead."

She jerked her hands out of his. "You're crazy."

He smiled. "About you? Certainly."

That was as much a lie as those blasted glasses of his. Knowing that steadied her. "How did you find me?"

"When I arrived I asked about you, and was told you were here. This is a friendly town, isn't it?"

"No, I meant—" Jane shook her head, trying to think. She knew how he'd found her. She had told him her name and her hometown. That was why she'd been afraid of the phone for the past three weeks; but she had never, ever expected him to show up like this.

Someone tugged at her arm. Dazed, Jane looked over at her friend. Liza looked torn between hurt and fascination. "Jane, who *is* this?"

She opened her mouth. And closed it again, before hysterical laughter could escape. Who was he? She had no idea.

"Samuel Charmaneaux," the man beside her said. "And I look forward to getting to know you, but right now— Well, as you can see, Jane wasn't expecting me." He looked around at the members of their interested audience, and his smile was a work of art—slightly abashed, yet confident. "I have some fences to mend, and if you ladies and gentlemen will excuse us, I can do that better once I have Jane to myself."

His arm urged her forward. She stumbled a few steps in automatic compliance before she realized what she was doing, and stopped. "You can't do this."

"Ah, sweetheart." He captured her face in his two hands and looked into her eyes. "We have so much to discuss, but that's why I'm here. We couldn't settle things over the phone and you weren't able to come to me, so I came to you. Are you angry that I didn't let you know I was coming?"

He really *was* crazy. "I don't know what you're doing here."

"You will." He bent his head. His lips brushed her ear, just as they had once before, when he had whispered that he would rather not kill the soldier who was looking for her. Then he whispered five magic words: "I didn't use a condom."

He drove a black Jeep Cherokee. That made sense to Jane. Black was the color of mystery, and Jeeps were for rugged people who crossed deserts, mountains…and tropical forests.

What didn't make sense was the way she allowed him to steer her away from everyone and toward his vehicle.

It was his hand on her arm that had done it, she decided. Her body had no sense. It had gotten used to following him. The rest of her knew better, only somehow here she stood, next to his vehicle. "My car is over there," she said, pulling away from him. "I need to drive it home. I'll follow you to wherever you're staying and we—we can talk." She admitted reluctantly, privately, that they did have to talk.

"Everyone expects us to ride home together. We'll excite less curiosity if we do what they expect."

She glared at him. "What you've *arranged* for them to expect, you mean."

"The longer we stand here and argue, the more curious your friends will become. How long do you think it will be before one of them comes over to see what's wrong?"

She didn't want that. She didn't want him here at all, but he was, and she had to deal with it, which meant she had to avoid answering any questions about him until they could get their stories straight. She had no idea what he'd told everyone while he was waiting for her.

Without speaking, she turned and climbed into his Cherokee. When she closed the door, shutting herself up in the darkness, she had to swallow against the panic that lumped up in her throat. She felt like a mouse that had just crawled into the tiger's cage. She huddled deeper into her coat, colder now than when she had been outside.

He rounded the hood and opened his door.

"I'll go with you," she said, "but just so we can get a few things straight."

"An admirable goal." He sounded serious enough, yet she got an impression of underlying amusement in his tone, and that irritated her. He got in and closed his door with a solid-sounding thunk. "Fasten your seat belt, Jane."

"We can just drive around. We don't have to—to go anywhere." Like to his motel room. Now that she thought about it, she definitely didn't want to go there. "You're staying at the Friendly Inn, I imagine?" Atherton only had two motels, and she couldn't picture this man choosing to stay at the other one, which rented more rooms by the hour than by the night.

"I passed it on the way in." When he turned the key, the car's heater started, along with the engine. He punched in a tape and the low, bluesy sound of a sax filled the car like an echo of the night outside.

Maybe it was her need to drown out the sad wail of that sax that made her start chattering like an idiot. "If you haven't checked into the motel yet, you'll need to do that before midnight. They don't keep the desk open any later. But this shouldn't take long. We can drive around and talk, and then you can bring me back here." That would work. Everyone would have gone home, and she could get in her car and go home, too. The image of her cozy living room hovered at the edge of her mind like a promise of safety. "I'll need my car to get to work in the morning."

He sighed and leaned one arm on the steering wheel, turning to face her. "Some things are easier to say in the dark, it's true. But 'easy' isn't always best. I think we should have our conversation face-to-face, Jane. That's one reason I came instead of calling."

She gave him a quick, alarmed glance. "But you'll bring me back here after we talk."

"If that's what you want. I'm hoping it won't be."

She stiffened. "If you're planning to pick up where you left off—"

"No. That's not why I'm here."

"Why *are* you here?" she demanded.

"To find out if you are carrying my child."

Five

"I'm not."

She said it quickly. Too quickly? Samuel couldn't tell. His usual detachment failed him again, as it had so often with this woman. He'd spent years building the mental calluses necessary to do his job, years cultivating the detachment he'd needed to survive—but his calluses had been ripped off the day Jack had died. Nothing had been the same since, and Samuel couldn't trust his impressions when the answer mattered so much.

The Cherokee had an automatic transmission, so he was able to rest his aching left hand while he put the vehicle in gear. He kept his foot on the brake, not willing to go forward until she answered his question. "So you're not pregnant? You're sure of this?"

The pale light from the streetlamp fell across her face, leaching it of color and leaving the rest of her in shadow. "I can't be p-pregnant." Her hands clutched at each other in her lap. "I just can't be."

"You mean you don't want to be." Relief hit him hard, making his middle hollow and his head light. He still had a chance. He took his foot off the brake and pulled out into the quiet street. "But you aren't sure. If you were, you wouldn't have come with me when I mentioned not using a condom."

She didn't answer. Let her have her silence for now, he thought. He had something far more important—something he hadn't had in years, though he'd only recently realized he needed it. He had hope.

Jane waited tensely for him to continue questioning her. Surely he hadn't come all the way to Atherton to ask her once, then drop the subject. Of course, she didn't know how far he'd come, did she? She didn't know anything about him. "Where are you from?" she asked suddenly.

"I was born in Chicago," he said easily. "But I haven't lived there since I was three years old."

"Where are you from *now?*"

"I haven't had a fixed residence in several years."

"But you have to live somewhere. Everyone lives somewhere!"

"People in my former occupation often don't, Jane."

Former occupation? She swallowed and glanced at him. In the faint glow from the dash lights, he looked enticing and remote. A stray bit of light glinted off the metal rims of his glasses—those lying glasses that proclaimed him to be all sorts of things he wasn't. Like safe. Knowable. Part of a world she could understand.

His hands, though... One hand gripped the steering wheel. The other rested on his thigh. The sight of them both troubled and reassured her, because she knew those hands. In ways she didn't want to remember, she knew them. They were the one thing about him that stayed the same, no matter who he was pretending to be. "Is your name really Samuel Charmaneaux?"

He didn't look away from the road. "It is now."

What kind of answer was that? How was she supposed to deal with this man? Dammit, she didn't *want* to deal with him. She wanted him to go away again. He'd done that once—left without a word. And it had hurt; it had hurt far more than it should have.

Why couldn't he have stayed gone?

"There aren't very many cars on the street," he said suddenly. "And the restaurant on the corner looks closed."

She blinked, surprised. "Well, it's after ten. Green's stops serving at ten."

He smiled. "Do the streets roll up at ten o'clock on weekdays in Atherton?"

"Oh, no. There are a couple of bars that stay open late, and the truck stop is open all night. And the late movie doesn't get out for a couple of hours." She paused. "I guess that doesn't sound like much, if you're used to cities like Chicago."

"I told you, I haven't lived there since I was three. I'm adaptable." The light was red. As he pulled to a stop at the intersection, he looked around with apparent fascination.

"What's so interesting?"

"Your town."

She didn't know what he was talking about. They were on the fringes of the business section; to the left was a gas station, while the other corners were held down by a drugstore, an old house that had been converted to doctors' offices, and a small church. Just ahead were some of the oldest houses in Atherton—big old houses with long verandas that were shaded in summer by trees that had seen the century in.

But it wasn't summer, and spring's early dusting of green didn't show in the dark. Tonight those ancient trees were gaunt shadows whose limbs formed skeleton shapes against the night sky. Jane shivered and cursed her imagination. "I guess this isn't the sort of place you're used to."

"No, it isn't." The traffic light changed, and they pulled

away from it. "What's that building?" He indicated a two-story brick house on their left. The discreet floodlights and the small sign, unreadable from this angle, were the only indications it wasn't a private dwelling.

"The new library. It used to be the Fraser place. The family donated it to the city about five years ago." Was this his idea of small talk? Somehow she didn't think so. Everything this man did seemed imbued with purpose.

"Do you know everyone here?"

"Not everyone, no. Of course not. Atherton isn't *that* small. But I grew up here, and now that I'm teaching, I come in contact with a lot of people."

"And you know the stories that go with the places here."

"Well...yes. Mostly."

"That's good." A small smile played over his lips. "Yes, this seems like a very pleasant little town. I noticed a number of retail stores. Do most people in Atherton shop locally?"

"I—yes, I suppose we do, for most things. I mean, sometimes people drive into Kansas City for the malls, make a weekend of it, but— Why on earth do you want to know that?"

"It's important to a town's economic health that people support their local merchants," he said seriously. "Census data indicate that Atherton is hanging on to a fair percentage of its young people, which is an important predictor for continued growth, but hardly the only one."

Jane closed her gaping mouth. For the next few blocks, she worried so hard over what he'd said and what he hadn't said that she didn't notice where they were. "Surely," she said at last, "you aren't planning on staying in Atherton long enough for any of this to matter to you. I mean, a man in your, uh, profession wouldn't find a lot to do here."

"Have you decided what my profession is, then?" He sounded amused. "I had the impression you had some doubts."

"You're definitely not James Bond."

He chuckled. That quiet sound surprised her. It also made her remember. He'd chuckled just like that when she'd reacted with such horror over the idea that he might be a herpetologist. She remembered other things, too. She was so busy trying not to remember those things that she didn't realize where they were until the Jeep slowed. They turned into a driveway that led to an old frame house where a porch light glowed at the upstairs landing.

Her porch light. "This is my apartment!" She felt betrayed—by whom or what, she wasn't sure.

"I told you I'd asked about you. Your landlady was very helpful." He pulled up where she always parked, next to the foot of the outside stairway at the side of the house.

"Frances Ann told you where I was?" Jane sat rigid, disbelieving. Frances Ann MacAllister called the sheriff about prowlers whenever dogs tipped over the garbage cans. She was not a trusting soul.

"I told her I was your fiancé."

"You *what?*" Outrage cut through several layers of confusion. "How could you do that to me? Do you have any idea what kind of questions I'm going to face? How much trouble you've made for me?"

"Jane." He reached out and took her hand. Just like that, heat slid into her, sweet, beckoning, unwanted. "I don't want to cause you trouble. Truly. But won't it be harder to explain being pregnant if you don't have a fiancé?"

"I'm not... I don't..." Her voice faded as her innate honesty fought with the need to deny what she feared. It was possible. She wanted to believe her last period had been so skimpy because of stress, but her sister-in-law had experienced exactly the same thing in the first month she was pregnant with Charlie. She'd tried not to think about it. Thinking about it meant admitting just how foolishly she'd behaved. It meant contemplating the possibility of telling her mother she was pregnant by a man whose name she didn't know.

But that man wasn't unknown anymore. He had a name. Or at least, he said that Samuel was his name…now.

Jane used her free hand to push her hair out of her face. In spite of the crackers and the occasional queasiness and the fact that her last period had been extremely light, she couldn't believe she was pregnant. Stress could upset a woman's stomach as well as her menstrual cycle. Or maybe she was allergic to something. Or maybe she had brought back some disgusting parasite from her island adventure. Or maybe…

Samuel stroked his thumb over the back of her hand. "I'm going to do what I can to make things easier for you, Jane."

Suddenly, anything—even having this man in her apartment—seemed better than sitting here in the close, quiet darkness with him, hearing him say her name that way. "Hot chocolate," she blurted, and threw open the car door. "Let's go upstairs. I'll make us some hot chocolate."

She couldn't get up those stairs fast enough. Unfortunately, what she was trying to run from followed her, light-footed and silent. Jane's hand disgusted her by shaking slightly as she put her key in the lock. This was ridiculous. He had her so rattled she wasn't thinking straight. She was scarcely thinking at all. She took a deep breath, opened her door and felt for the light switch. "Listen, I have some questions I want answered, and I want— Omigosh." She stopped one foot into her living room, staring at the two large leather suitcases sitting in the center of her braided rug. "Where did those come from?"

"They're mine." Samuel put his hands on her shoulders and moved her gently aside, then stepped in after her and pulled her door closed, locking it.

"How did they get in here?" she demanded. "I know Frances Ann didn't open the door for you, no matter what you told her!"

"When you didn't answer your door, I let myself in. It seemed the simplest way to establish my bona fides with your landlady," he explained.

"You didn't have a key."

His mouth turned up at one corner. "That wasn't a problem."

He had let himself in. Without a key. Because it had seemed simplest. Of course. She paced a few steps away, turned and frowned at him. "Well, you can just carry them back downstairs and out to your car, because there is no way you are staying here."

"You are more familiar with what is customary in Atherton than I am, of course, but I thought that even in a small town it might seem odd for a woman's fiancé to stay at a motel, rather than with her."

Jane pictured herself tossing his suitcases out the door and watching them thud-thud-thud down the stairs. The image was satisfying. The scene her imagination conjured next, where the police showed up because Frances Ann had heard the thuds and called the cops, wasn't as appealing. "You are not my fiancé."

"I told your friends that I am." He drifted over to the couch, which sat away from the wall, facing the fireplace. His fingers slid along the quilt she kept on the back of the couch—a lovely old wedding-ring quilt Grandma Ellis had made before Jane was born. "I like your living room."

"It's nothing special." Her furniture was a hodgepodge of styles that didn't match, but managed a sort of peaceful coexistence. Most of the surfaces were a bit cluttered. Jane wasn't a real collector, but she was fond of objects with a history, like the toy locomotive that sat on the end table where her unwanted guest paused. Her father had played with that toy when he was a boy. Or like the framed photograph that Samuel was studying so intently—a picture of Jane and her two older brothers on the beach. She'd been seven when that photo was taken. They had driven all the way to Galveston, Texas, for vacation that year. It had been the first time she'd seen the ocean, and the last time they'd taken a trip as a whole family. Her parents had divorced three months later.

"The room suits you." He set down the photo. "You have a good eye."

"I— Thank you." She watched him make a slow circuit of the room, pausing in front of a framed circus poster.

"The Great Bandini," he said thoughtfully, looking at the faded image of a man on a tightrope. "Was that your father's circus name?"

She was beyond being surprised by anything he said or did. "How did you know?"

He slid her one of those considering glances. "I know quite a bit about you, Jane. This *is* a poster advertising one of your father's performances, isn't it?"

She nodded. Later, she told herself, she would tackle the questions about how he knew about Papa. First things first. "Why did you tell everyone we were engaged?"

He stopped in front of the entertainment center that held her TV and stereo. "It was a good reason for me to come here, and I needed somewhere to go. Is this the only sound system you have?"

Her eyebrows went up. "You have a problem with it?"

He just gave her that half smile that made her knees silly.

She frowned. "Stop changing the subject. Someone like you must have a hundred places to go that are more interesting than Atherton. Unless—" Her imagination jumped in with a frightening possibility. "Oh, God. Are you on the run from the police? Or from—"

He chuckled. "No, nothing like that. I'm…retired."

Relief was altogether too short-lived. Retired from what? She'd been avoiding pressing him for an answer to that question far too long. It couldn't be put off anymore. She steadied herself. "I think it's time you told me exactly what you were doing on San Tomás."

"I can't tell you that. Not exactly. But I'm not a criminal, if that's what you're wondering."

"Am I supposed to take your word on that?"

"Basically. I can offer you evidence to support my story, but frankly, you wouldn't be able to tell if it's real or not. Some fakes are so good, even the experts are confused."

Jane had a sense of standing on the edge of some precipice, and she wanted to step back. She wasn't a woman who handled risks well, so she *would* have stepped back right away— if only she'd been sure where the stupid edge was. "So what is this story of yours?"

"Until three weeks ago, I was an operative for a covert government agency."

"A spy."

"If you like."

"What are you now?"

"Unemployed." His smile was an invitation she didn't want to interpret. "May we have that hot chocolate now?"

She ignored that. "Samuel, why are you here?"

"I told you."

Jane was not good at confrontation, but she set her shoulders and persisted. "I don't think you've told me everything."

He shrugged. "I suppose I have more than one reason. Aren't most people's motives mixed, most of the time?" He started toward her. "I'd hoped you wouldn't mind seeing me again, that you might even like it. You're angry, though, aren't you? And nervous." When he stopped in front of her, he was standing too close. It messed up her breathing for him to be this near her. "Pretty Jane, is it so terrible to see me again?"

"No, not terrible. I just— You—" She stuttered to stop, worried that she might have hurt his feelings. But, damn it, she shouldn't be concerned about his feelings when he'd shown so little consideration for hers. "You're right. I *am* angry. You didn't even say goodbye."

He blinked, as if she'd surprised him. "If I tell you it didn't occur to me, that will indict me pretty thoroughly in your eyes, won't it?" His smile twisted. "When your life is temporary, Jane, you don't say goodbye to people any more than you say goodbye to the sun when it sets. Leaving people and places behind becomes as normal and unnoticed as exhaling."

"That's an awful way to live."

His gaze sharpened, the blue of his eyes was suddenly more intense. "Maybe you can teach me another way to live."

Oh, no. No, she wasn't the sort of woman who could teach this man anything. She took a deep breath. "About what happened between us…"

He smiled. "Yes?"

When had he moved? He was so close now, she had to tilt her head back to continue to meet his gaze. "It's not going to happen again."

"No?" He sounded only mildly interested. "I suppose you think I took advantage of you."

"Didn't you?"

"I was as caught up in what happened as you were."

For a second, she believed him. The possibility that she had had such an effect on this man was dizzying. Then he spoke, and all her daring washed away. "You don't have to worry. I won't lose control again. Don't frown so, pretty Jane." He brushed a kiss across her cheek. "I'm in control now. I won't do anything you don't want me to do. May I stay here with you tonight?"

She jerked back. "What?"

"On your couch, of course." His eyes mocked her. "It's late, and I've had a long drive. I'm tired."

"No. No, that wouldn't be a good idea. I've got to get up early, and—and I wasn't expecting company. I don't have anything at home for breakfast. That sofa is really not very comfortable, and—"

"I know you weren't expecting company, and I don't care

about breakfast or your couch. It's bound to be better than some of the places I've slept.''

She felt a twinge of sympathy, but sternly suppressed it. "I don't think we've settled anything. I still don't know anything about you, or why you're here.''

"I've answered everything you've asked me.''

She must not be asking the right questions. One loomed in her mind now: *Why hadn't he called?* When she realized that was the one question above all others she needed answered, it frightened her. That question shouldn't be so important. It wasn't as if she was in love with the man. "We'll talk more tomorrow. *If* you're still in Atherton.''

"I'm not going anywhere.''

"You're going to the motel.''

"Trying to hustle me out without my hot chocolate? Unfair.'' He did look tired. There was strain on his face, a deep-seated weariness she tried to steel herself against. "Listen, Jane,'' he said, grasping her arm. The flinch of his eyes was so slight she almost missed it. He dropped his hand.

"What is it? What's wrong?''

"Nothing.'' He held his hand waist-high, opening and closing it slowly. This was the first time she'd gotten a good look at his left hand. There was a puckered scab along the back of it. Impulsively she reached out and took his hand in both of hers. "My God, Samuel, what happened?''

"I was careless.'' He sounded distracted. "It happened after I left you.''

Jane cradled his hand in both of hers, unconsciously stroking the undamaged part of his palm with one finger. "It looks like something went right through it.''

"A knife,'' he said, standing very still.

"Someone *stabbed* you?''

"Occupational hazard. I'm all right.'' There was an odd note in his voice.

She looked up and met his gaze. Her breath caught. Oh, no, she thought. No. If she could persuade herself his eyes didn't make her dizzy, that the warmth of his skin didn't make her own skin feel hot and tight, she'd be okay. If she could make herself believe those things, maybe he would believe them, too. "You can sleep on the couch," she said, and was so caught in the tropical blue of his eyes that she didn't even notice his glasses. "I'll get you a pillow."

Samuel loved showers. He liked the spray of water in his face and down his back, and he liked the water hot. He knew exactly when his love for long, hot showers had started. He'd been twelve when he'd lived with Betty and Stan Freedman. Betty had persuaded him that cleanliness wasn't just a chore, but a way of feeling good about himself.

After Stan's heart attack, the social-services people had moved him and the two other foster children living with the Freedmans to other homes. He'd only been with them for a short time, yet he had grieved. It had been the first time in years he had grieved over a parting, and the last.

Until Jack had died.

For the past couple of years, Samuel had known something was wrong, but he hadn't known what. He'd been conscious only of feeling...thin. Shadowy. Not quite real. Then Jack had died, and, oddly enough, the grief he'd felt for his friend had made Samuel feel real again. That was when he'd known he had to leave the agency, to find what he'd known so briefly with the Freedmans—an ordinary life, filled with ordinary people; people who knew him by name, who remembered things he'd said or done in the past; people who mattered, because they were part of his life. It would take time to build those connections, but he knew how to be patient.

Standing in Jane's shower, letting the hot water pour over him, Samuel felt thoroughly real. She had let him stay. He smiled as he lathered his stomach. For some reason, he'd been reluctant to use his wound to elicit her sympathy, keeping that as a last resort, but it had worked. He'd known it would.

What he hadn't known was how he would feel when her eyes went soft with distress over his damaged hand. The feelings had been unsettling, but pleasant. It had been a long time since anyone had fussed over him.

He decided he liked it.

Samuel lingered in Jane's shower for a long time, letting the heat and the water soothe him. He was here, and he could get her to give him what he wanted. He'd seen the heat in her eyes, however wary she felt about him. Jane might not want to want him, but she did.

He wanted her, too. The jolt of hunger he'd felt when he touched her had surprised him. He'd thought his response to her down on San Tomás had been a product of circumstances, but apparently not. He felt the same simmer of need here, in Atherton.

He could handle that—starting now, by switching from hot water to cold. As he reached out to turn the hot water off, he promised himself he wouldn't lose control again.

Jane preferred winter to summer because she loved to snuggle under the blankets. It was still chilly enough for blankets, so she lay on her side with her covers tucked up under her chin, just the way she liked them. But that night, her bed felt lonely, not cozy.

She could hear the shower running. Her uninvited guest had asked politely if it would bother her for him to take a shower tonight, and she, fool that she was, had said it wouldn't. Now she lay awake in her double bed, staring into the darkness and listening to him take a shower, and she felt so alone she ached with it—and with other feelings. Feelings flavored with memories, spicy with temptation and risk. And, dammit, she knew why her foolish body kept reacting to the idea of him in the shower, but why would a sound that made it clear she *wasn't* alone make her feel so lonely?

Life was so unfair. Her emotions didn't make any sense, her body couldn't be trusted, and her mind wasn't in much better shape. It kept repeating the same questions over and over again.

He said he wanted to know if she carried his child.

Was that really why he was here? Who was he? Was he thinking about her right now? He had been awfully determined to stay here, with her. Maybe he couldn't get her out of his mind, just as she— No, she told herself, rolling over and punching her pillow into a new shape. She was not going to let her imagination do this to her. If Samuel lay awake tonight, it would be because his hand was hurting.

His poor hand. If she hadn't seen that, she wouldn't have let him stay. Funny that he'd tried to use it just when she was about to get him out of here. Almost as if— No, surely not. His reaction when he'd tried to use his bad hand had been too subtle to be an act. No, he hadn't used his injury to get sympathy so that she'd let him stay. The idea was far-fetched.

Almost as far-fetched as the idea that he really was—or had been—a spy.

Did she believe him?

Maybe. Jane rolled onto her back and turned her pillow over onto the cool side. Those damned glasses, she thought. They reminded her that he was as changeable as a chameleon. Even if she believed him about the spy stuff, she couldn't rid herself of a nagging feeling that he still hadn't told her the whole truth about why he was here.

Maybe he really did want her. Maybe he hadn't been able to forget her. Maybe...

She threw her pillow onto the floor.

Six

Her alarm didn't go off.

As soon as her eyes drifted open and she saw the accusing red glare of the LED on her clock, Jane jumped out of bed. She was never late. Flustered, she forgot everything else and threw open the bedroom door while still in her pajamas— bright red thermal long johns.

She stopped two feet from her door, and two inches from Samuel's chest.

"Good morning," he said, smiling at her from the doorway to the living room. He wore sweats. The old, baggy-at-the-knees garments made him look as close to ordinary as a man with a perfect body, to-die-for blue eyes and a killer smile could look. His hair was tied back as neatly as always. Even when he'd been escaping guerrillas, his hair had stayed in that neat ponytail. "I hope you don't mind that I made myself at home in your kitchen. I've got coffee ready."

The thought of hot coffee nearly seduced her into forgiving him for looking so good when her hair was all over the place

and she was wearing the world's unsexiest pj's. They had
feet in them, for crying out loud. "Later." She gulped, and
turned and fled for the bathroom.

She might have forgotten to set her alarm last night, but
at least she'd remembered to hang her clothes in the bathroom. The outfit she'd chosen was one of her favorite mood-
boosters. The sweater was Easter-egg blue, and the knit of
the matching pants was so soft it made her want to pet her
leg when she wore them.

Not that anyone was going to be petting her leg, she assured herself hastily as she added a touch of blush to her
cheeks. She'd dressed purely for herself, not because she
wanted to impress anyone. She added a little lipstick, took a
deep breath and opened the bathroom door. And heard
voices. The first voice she heard was Samuel's. It was the
second one that made her groan aloud. Some mornings, it
just didn't pay to get up.

Her mother was here.

Samuel had been glad Jane was still in the shower when
her mother had knocked on the door. It had given him time
to make the right impression. Fortunately, the quilt and pillow
he'd used last night were still on the couch. After he'd let
Mrs. Smith in, he'd paused to fold the quilt before taking her
into the kitchen for coffee, making a point about where he'd
slept last night without saying a word.

It hadn't taken him long to see what Marilee Smith wanted
in a prospective son-in-law—a harmless, conventional man
with a respectable job. He knew how to project that image.
By the time Jane joined them, her mother was liking him
very well indeed.

"Mama," Jane said from the doorway, sounding flustered.
"It's awfully early for you to drop by."

Samuel looked at Jane and smiled. He liked seeing her in
that gentle shade of blue. The sweater was oversize and the

pants weren't tight, but her hips and pretty, round bottom gave the soft knit a delicious shape.

He remembered cupping her bottom in his two hands.

Hunger closed down on him like the jaws of a trap, too quick and too hard. He picked up his mug and sipped coffee to give himself a moment to recover.

"I don't suppose there's any one time when I can visit my daughter," Marilee Smith said.

"No, of course not, but I can't remember you ever coming over before eight o'clock in the morning."

"How else am I going to see you? You have to be at the school so early."

"You might have tried coming over after work," Jane said dryly. She crossed to the counter and poured a cup of coffee, then frowned at it without drinking.

"It's decaf, I'm afraid," Samuel said gently. "Either you're out of the regular or I couldn't find it."

"It tastes just fine," Jane's mother assured him. Marilee Smith was a pleasant woman whom the years had faded. Her hair was an indeterminate color, neither brown nor gray. She wore a "nice" pantsuit in a "nice," neutral color, and her oversize glasses magnified the faintly worried expression in her eyes as she regarded her daughter.

She was, Samuel thought, the sort of woman people met and forgot within the same hour. Part of him admired such relentless anonymity. He wondered what she was hiding from.

Jane didn't join them at the table. She leaned against the counter, sipping her coffee and hugging her other arm protectively around her middle. "We won't have much time to visit. I have to leave in a few minutes."

Her mother frowned. "Are you wearing that cheap old necklace your father gave you? Really, dear, I know you're attached to it, but you need to present a more professional image at work."

Jane's hand went to the little locket at her neck. She

flushed and quickly tucked it inside the sweater. "It's not cheap."

Samuel remembered seeing that necklace against her skin when she had lain beneath him on the forest floor. Jane was right. It wasn't cheap. It was apparently a source of conflict between the two women, however. He stood and smiled. "Can I get you some more coffee, Mrs. Smith?"

"Thank you, Samuel. You may freshen mine." Marilee Smith gave him an approving nod. When she turned to her daughter, her expression changed, drooping sadly. "Just how long did you intend to wait before you introduced me to your fiancé?"

"Mama, he just got here last night, and anyway—"

"I was shocked when I heard about him, Jane. Shocked and hurt. I've always said you can tell me anything." She paused. *"Anything."*

Samuel wondered as he retrieved the coffeepot what heinous deeds the woman suspected might fall under that blanket permission. He had thought he'd eased her maternal anxieties pretty well, but he'd noticed that her daughter's imagination tended toward the lurid. Maybe it ran in the family.

Jane bit her lip. "Mama, Samuel isn't exactly my fiancé."

He spoke quickly. "Jane, I've explained to your mother that you and I aren't seeing eye-to-eye on everything right now, including the, uh, status of our relationship." He brought the coffeepot over to the table. "Jane is worried that everything happened too quickly with us, Mrs. Smith."

"Do call me Marilee," she said, holding out her cup.

"Marilee," he repeated obediently as he poured her coffee. "I have to respect Jane's qualms. We met on vacation, after all, and we hadn't known each other long before she made that ill-fated trip to the interior of the island and we were separated. However certain I am of my own feelings, she deserves time to be sure of hers."

The choking sound behind him came from Jane.

"But she didn't say anything," Marilee Smith said. "She never even mentioned you."

"I'm a rather private person. I'm sure Jane was trying to respect that." He smiled as he resumed his seat. "She told me a great deal about you." He would have no trouble backing up that claim, since the report he'd received on Jane had included information on her family, including the fact that her parents had been divorced when her father, the tightrope walker, was killed in a traffic accident.

He found he was very curious about Jane's father.

"Did she?" Marilee almost let herself be distracted by that, but doggedly returned to her point. "Still, I can't believe you would have objected to her telling me about you. You've been very open with me. And surely you were just as open with your own parents."

"I'm afraid my parents died several years ago."

Jane muttered something under her breath. It sounded like "How convenient." Samuel's lips twitched in amusement. His sweet Jane didn't believe much of anything he said— even the parts that were true.

"Oh, I'm so sorry." Jane's mother patted his hand. "Do you have brothers or sisters?"

"There's just me."

"Mama," Jane said firmly, "stop grilling Samuel."

"You can hardly blame me if I have a few questions, since you haven't seen fit to tell me anything."

"I didn't know what to say—" she shot Samuel a dirty look "—since everything is so unresolved."

"You might have mentioned that you were considering marriage. I didn't even know he existed until Teresa Goodman called me. Of course, Teresa didn't know much, either. She didn't even know that Samuel is a professor." She gave Samuel an approving glance.

Jane hadn't known that, either, of course. Until now. Samuel spoke quickly. "Not a professor at the moment. Like I told you, I'm between jobs."

"Oh, but with your credentials, I'm sure Atherton College will snap you right up." Marilee beamed at him. "It's so sweet, the way you've uprooted yourself and come all this way to be with Jane."

Samuel knew Jane didn't think it was sweet at all. Storm warnings flashed in her eyes, and her mouth was pressed tight to hold in all the things she wanted to say to him. He set down his mug and stood. "Jane, we should be going, or there won't be time to take you by the bank to pick up your car."

"Omigosh, I'd forgotten. Mama, I'm sorry, but I do have to rush." She looked more relieved than sorry. Apparently she considered riding with him the lesser of two evils.

"Where is your car, dear? At the bank? That's what Teresa told me when she called this morning. She said you drove off with Samuel right after that meeting." Marilee stood. "I'll take you to get it. No point in making Samuel go out."

"He doesn't mind," Jane said brightly. "Really. Let's go, Samuel."

Her mother paid no attention to this weak attempt to divert her. "Now, Samuel, you and Jane will have to come to dinner this Friday so you can meet the boys and their wives. They're dear girls," she said, starting for the living room. "And the children are so sweet. You do like children, don't you?"

"Of course," he murmured, staying at her side. "Here, let me help you with your coat." He lifted it from the coatrack and held it for her.

"Wonderful." She beamed at him. "Jane? Didn't you say you were running late? Don't dally."

Jane gave him one long, deadly look and reached for her coat. Samuel suspected she was in for a major interrogation once her mother got her alone. No doubt Jane was wondering what to say about the man she was supposedly engaged to, when her mother knew more of his story than she did.

He smiled at her. "Your collar is crooked, sweetheart." He moved to stand in front of her, his body blocking her mother's view. Jane glared up at him while he adjusted her

collar, his fingers lingering to brush the nape of her neck. He
felt the goose bumps that shivered over her, and was pleased.
"Mrs. Smith," he said, looking down into the anger and
confusion in Jane's eyes, "I hope you don't mind if I kiss
your daughter goodbye."

Marilee said coyly that she would wait for Jane on the
landing, and opened the door. Cold air with the sharp, pre-
monitory taste of rain blew in.

"How could you do this to me?" Jane hissed as the door
closed. "She's going to ask me all kinds of questions about
you. What am I supposed to say?"

"That's why I arranged a moment of privacy for
us...sweetheart. So I could tell you." When she got really
angry, he noticed, her eyes brightened, becoming almost to-
paz—the same color they had turned when he was inside her.

He moved his hands from her collar to her shoulders to
keep himself from sliding them inside her coat and cupping
her breasts. "I'm a teacher, just like you. That's what brought
us together on the cruise. Until recently I taught history at a
small private college in New Hampshire. I'm thirty-one, have
never been married, and have been to South America twice
on work-study trips connected with my area of expertise,
Latin American history. My minor was Asian studies. I'm
looking for a position here in Atherton, or nearby."

"And what do I tell her about your hand? Did one of your
students object to the grade you gave him?"

Startled, he froze. He'd forgotten his hand. He'd been so
distracted by his growing desire, he'd failed to finish briefing
her. "An accident with an awl," he said, frowning at his
uncharacteristic lapse. "I'm not particularly handy with
tools."

Her gaze searched his. "And is any of that true?" she
whispered.

Samuel looked at the tension that tightened her face and
made a decision. He wasn't going to lie to this woman. He
might not always be able to tell her the truth, but he wouldn't

tell an outright lie. "I have been to South America, and I am looking for a job."

"Here in Atherton?"

He saw more questions in her eyes than just the one she spoke aloud. Suddenly he was impatient with questions, with the need to balance his answers between his promise to himself not to lie and his determination to get what he wanted from her. He bent and brushed his lips across hers to quiet her.

It worked. She went still, the way a small, wild creature might at the edge of a clearing. He knew he couldn't push her too far. She was right to be wary. But her taste was sweet, too sweet for that brief contact to be enough, and he went back for more.

Her lips quivered beneath his, then opened. And Samuel got lost. Lost in the taste of her. Lost in the desire that rose, smoky and hot, in his own body. Lost in the way she responded to him, letting his tongue test hers while her hands held on to his arms as if he were the only fixed point in her universe.

When he tightened his hands on her shoulders, the pain that shot through his injured palm wasn't enough to stop him. But it reminded him that he had to stop. He straightened, looking down into her eyes—wide, startled eyes, as pretty as the sun-dappled ground where they had once lain together.

It was all he could do to release her and step back.

Neither of them spoke. She stared at him for another second, then turned and fumbled for the door. An instant later, she was gone.

Samuel stood quietly, waiting for the storm in his body to subside. He could make no sense of his response, and after a moment he quit trying.

It wasn't a bad thing, surely, to want the woman he intended to marry.

Her cordless phone was in the kitchen. He got the handset and punched in a series of numbers, waited for the count of five, then punched in another, longer set of numbers, waited again and punched in the number he was calling from. Then he disconnected and carried the handset with him back to the living room.

He would wait twenty minutes to see if his former superior wanted to contact him. That gave him time to learn more about the woman who might be carrying his child.

The homey hodgepodge of her living room intrigued him. Samuel lingered by the crowded entertainment center, whose shelves were filled with books and the colorful odds and ends Jane had collected. He knelt to take a better look at her stereo, and grimaced. It was every bit as inadequate as he'd thought when he'd glanced at it last night. Music was one of the few luxuries that mattered to him. Samuel didn't own many things, but he had a very good stereo in storage that he intended to have shipped here as soon as possible. He would have to wait, though. Jane hadn't accepted him as a part of her life. Not yet.

He couldn't be sure she was going to accept him at all, of course. Except sexually. She wanted him, and he knew more about seduction than she did. He didn't doubt he would be able to have her again. He was uncharacteristically impatient about it, in fact.

But he needed more from her than her body.

Her shelves held an interesting assortment of objects. She liked fiction just fine when it came between the covers of a book, he noted wryly, and preferred romance and fantasy. That didn't surprise him, and he could account for the odds and ends of circus memorabilia because of her father.

But not all of her possessions fit neatly into his picture of her. Like the Red Cross booklets tucked into one corner of the bookcase. It appeared she had taken a number of courses involving first aid or disaster relief. That intrigued him. In his experience, civilians believed they lived in a safe world and seldom prepared themselves for disaster.

The phone rang. He straightened, pressed the button and said his current name.

"So, how are you liking Kansas? Ready to come back to the real world yet?" a familiar gravelly voice said into his ear.

Samuel chuckled. Only Patrick Hayes would refer to the subterranean world of covert operations as the "real" world. "I'm retired, remember?"

"You're bound to come to your senses sooner or later," Patrick replied confidently. "In the meantime, I have a little favor I'd like to discuss."

"No." Samuel spoke without hesitation, in spite of what he owed this man. Without Hayes's help, Samuel couldn't have stepped out of his old life as cleanly as he had. Not everyone connected with the agency had wanted Samuel to retire. "Besides, wouldn't my reappearance complicate matters? I'm supposed to be dead."

"Not if you aren't a permanent employee. I've got more leeway about what goes in the records on a freelancer. And I need you for this one," he said, all humor dropping from his voice. "I wouldn't ask if I didn't."

Samuel did hesitate this time. He liked Hayes; he owed him for a lot more than his new identity. But that part of the debt was complicated and hardly one-sided. Ten years ago, Hayes had recruited him for the agency, giving him a place to belong and a chance to make a difference. Ten years ago, Samuel had needed both things. But along the way he'd come too close to becoming a shadow himself, no more real than the identities he put on and sloughed off with every assignment. "I can't, Patrick."

The other man was silent for only a second before saying cheerfully, "Well, hell, are you still holding that little problem with your hand against me?"

The knot of obligation in Samuel's chest loosened. "San Tomás *was* supposed to be the last favor, remember?"

Patrick chuckled. "All right, all right, I had to try. So you're really planning to grow corn?"

"No, I'm planning to grow minds. It's called teaching."

Samuel finished investigating Jane's living area while he talked with a man who was almost a friend. Hayes couldn't be a real friend—not in the way that Jack had been; *his* first allegiance was to the agency. But they shared several interests, and Samuel enjoyed talking with him. Hayes didn't bring up the matter of favors again.

When they ended the call, Samuel went to the hallway. There was one room left to check—Jane's bedroom. He was curious about her most private space, and yet, when he had his hand on her doorknob, he hesitated. It wasn't respect for her privacy that stopped him; he'd spent too many years prying into areas people would kill to keep secret to be bothered by scruples of that sort.

No, he wanted Jane to invite him in. That was all. The desire was as strong as it was whimsical, and he couldn't tell where it came from. He was adaptable but not impulsive, and whimsy had never been part of his life…except to the extent that Jack had been part of his life. Jack had appreciated whimsy.

Still, what would it hurt to wait? Sooner or later, Jane would invite him into her bedroom, and he wanted that invitation. He wanted it very much.

He pulled his hand away from the door and went back into the living room, where he pulled on his running shoes. Later he planned to check out Atherton's YMCA, see what kind of equipment they had. Samuel's life had sometimes depended on the fitness of his body. It never occurred to him to neglect that, now that he was building himself an ordinary life.

But he didn't run to keep fit. Not really. That was a side benefit. Samuel ran because he needed to run, needed the effort and the exhaustion and the sheer circularity of an activity where he ended up, always, back where he had started.

In his first life, long before he became Samuel Charmaneaux, that sense of returning to his starting point over and over had been the one thing he had hated about running. Eventually, though, it had come to reassure him on some fundamental level. There was little enough to connect him to the boy who used to run because he had no other outlet for his emotions, and very little else in his life that he could control, except the demands he made on his own body.

At the front door he paused, looking back into Jane's cozy living room. The quilt he had slept beneath last night was laid neatly over the back of the couch. It was old, that quilt. It looked like an heirloom that had been passed down from one generation to the next, and it belonged in this room in a way he didn't fully understand—perhaps because *he* didn't belong here.

The yearning that rose in him was so old and familiar he scarcely noticed it.

The only place Samuel had ever belonged had been the agency, and eventually even that hadn't been the right place for him. But he was going to belong. Here, in Atherton. That was why he needed Jane. Through her, he could gain acceptance, become part of the life of this small town.

And if she *was* pregnant...if she carried a child, that child would bind her to him with bonds she would never be able to break. He stood very still and let the possibilities wash through him.

Hope wasn't an entirely comfortable feeling. But it was real. He closed the door quietly on his way out.

Seven

At 3:40 p.m. that afternoon, Jane threw her sixth-period students' tests into her satchel and hurried to her car. Normally she stayed for an hour or so after the bell rang. She liked to do some of her paperwork at the school so she would be available in case any of her students needed help. They did stop by, too, quite often, or sometimes another teacher would drop in to chat.

That was why she was in such a hurry today. Word had traveled fast about Samuel.

As she hurried across the parking lot, the sky was a sullen gray and the wind was huffing and puffing as if it meant to finally do something about the rain that had threatened all day. She sighed in relief as she slid behind the wheel of her little Toyota. It had been a difficult day, and not just because she'd had to scramble for answers to some of the questions people had asked.

She scowled as she lined up with the other cars exiting the parking lot. Everyone had been so blasted *amazed*. Enduring the astonishment on her friends' and colleagues' faces had turned out to be as hard as fielding their questions. Jane knew she was as ordinary as vanilla ice cream, and not exactly daring. Maybe she was the last person anyone would have expected to attract a man like Samuel. That didn't mean they all had to tell her so, with their expressions if not their words.

She didn't take her usual route home—not today. Some people communed with nature when they needed to restore their balance. Jane went to Second Street.

A few raindrops splattered on her windshield as she turned onto the street. Today she needed memories, hers and those that went back much further than she did. When her tires hit the section of the old road that was still brick, she smiled. The sound rumbled the tension from her shoulders. She loved this street. It was old and worn and beautiful. She'd walked to school along here when she was in the third grade, and her best friend had lived in the small frame house at the end of the block. The street dead-ended at the park her mother used to take her to, the one bordered by Fool's Creek. It had the best swings in the world.

Those memories were hers. The others—those belonged to the trees. The oaks on either side of her now had dreamed through more winters than anyone still living in Atherton, and it comforted her to see them, dark and nearly bare, their branches dusted with spring.

The splatters on her windshield turned into a sprinkle as she drove slowly along her favorite street. It was early for the storms that swept through Kansas every year, but nature didn't follow a strict timetable. She automatically flipped on the windshield wipers; just as automatically, she tuned in to a station that gave weather updates. Jane had a secret fascination for the extraordinary storms of spring, despite their destructive power.

The rain never quite materialized, though, and within a few blocks the sprinkle had stopped and a strip of blue rimmed the horizon. Apparently this particular storm would miss them. Jane switched the radio to a country-music channel and listened to a cowboy who had called home, but no one was there.

Would Samuel still be there when she got home?

She hoped not. She told herself that quite firmly as she approached the turnoff onto her street. He *ought* to be gone. She hadn't invited him to become a permanent guest. She hadn't invited him at all, and she should have made him leave this morning.

Only how could she have done it then? Her mother had sat there beaming at him, only too ready to welcome him into the family.

Tonight, though, Jane would be firm. Tonight, he was checking into a motel. He could stay in Atherton if that was what he wanted, but he wasn't staying with her.

As soon as she reached her block, she saw him. He stood in the front yard beneath the old elm, talking to Frances Ann and looking like the closest thing she'd ever seen to masculine perfection in a dark green sweater and jeans. A strand of hair had come loose from his ponytail and frisked around in the chilly wind.

Jane wanted to believe that the emotion making her heart jump around like crazy was anger, not relief or some absurd joy because he hadn't left. She wanted to just keep driving, right on past the house. She didn't, of course. Frances Ann would never forgive her if she didn't stop. So she pulled up in her drive, parked her car next to Samuel's black Jeep, took her courage in both hands and headed for the front of the house.

"What are you doing outside in this weather, Frances Ann?" Jane asked as cheerily as she could as she approached the other two.

"Your young man wanted me to look at this old tree," Frances Ann said in her quavery voice. "He thinks I should let him cut that dead limb off." She waved vaguely at the elm.

"Better for me to take it off than to wait and let a storm do it," Samuel said. "Mother Nature can be careless about where she leaves her things when she's finished playing with them, and we don't want that branch winding up in Jane's kitchen."

"You know how to trim tree limbs?" Jane raised her brows. "I thought you weren't very handy with tools."

His eyes smiled at her in a most unfair way, as if they were sharing a private joke. "I think I can manage."

"Such a nice young man," Frances Ann said. "I'm going to feel so much safer, having a man in the house again." She chattered on about how helpful he was. Apparently he had offered to take care of some other small chores for her.

Frances Ann was besotted, Jane thought glumly as she listened to her normally suspicious landlady sing Samuel's praises. Everyone adored the man. Even her mother. On the way to get Jane's car this morning, Marilee Smith had wanted to know what in the world was wrong with her daughter. Why was she dragging her feet when this incredible man— "a *professor*, Jane, and with such lovely manners"—wanted to marry her?

Was she the only one who could see past those gold-rimmed glasses to the dangerous man watching them all with cold blue eyes?

"We'd better let Frances Ann get out of this wind." Samuel glanced at Jane. "Besides, I have something to show you."

"Good idea," she said sweetly. "We do need to talk."

They went up the stairs together. There was just room enough on the staircase to do that, but it meant that his arm brushed hers with every step, so she dashed up the last few steps ahead of him.

"Frances Ann says she's heard someone messing around the house several times at night," he said from behind her.

"Frances Ann shouldn't live alone." Jane's heart was beating much too hard. She stuck her key in the door and decided she really had to start working out. Soon. "Her brother in Cincinnati has asked her to move in with him, but she won't. Lately she hears prowlers every time the wind blows."

She pushed open her door, slipped off her coat and tossed it on the couch. Taking a deep breath, she turned to face him. "Now, I don't know what you wanted to show me, but it can wait. I need to get some things clear between us."

"That's good, Jane. It's always best to understand exactly where you stand, isn't it?" He moved past her. "That's why I bought this. So we'll both know where we stand." He reached for a small box sitting next to the ivy that was trying to take over her coffee table. "Has it been at least two weeks since you missed your period?"

The box contained a home pregnancy test. She swallowed. "What makes you think I've—that I'm late?"

"If you'd had a full period since I left you on San Tomás, you wouldn't be worried about my failure to use a condom."

Jane was not used to discussing her monthly cycle with a man. Her cheeks flamed. I will not die of embarrassment, she told herself. I will not stutter or scream, either. She spoke slowly to keep herself from doing those things. "Where did you buy that?"

"At that charming little drugstore on Main. They have a soda fountain. I'd like to take you there sometime."

At Handy's Drugstore, in fact. Handy's, where Liza worked the register. Liza might be Jane's best friend, but she had no more sense of discretion than a four-year-old. "Do you realize what you've done? By this time tomorrow, half the people in town will know you bought a home pregnancy test." Her hands clenched into fists as realization struck. "My mother," she whispered. How long would it take this interesting fact to get back to her mother?

"I asked Liza not to tell anyone yet, since you haven't seen a doctor."

"If you think that will stop her—"

"For a few days, perhaps," he said calmly. "Jane, if you're pregnant, people are going to know."

"And if I'm not?" she demanded.

"Then we need to know that, don't we?"

She was suddenly, flamingly angry. "You can't stop pushing, can you? You talked me into letting you stay here last night. You manipulated my mother this morning and Frances Ann this afternoon with your soft voice and those stupid, lying glasses—and now you're pushing again, and I don't know why!"

She hardly knew what she was saying. She just knew she had to push back somehow. "Are you so anxious to be let off the hook? Okay." She spread her hands widely. "I hereby absolve you of all responsibility. If I am pregnant, I'll handle it just fine on my own."

He moved with such quick, deadly grace that she stepped back. Did he move like that around others? she wondered as her hand went to her throat, where her locket rested beneath her sweater. He must not. If he did, they'd never believe that safe image he projected.

"You misunderstand." He stopped in front of her, looming over her, with menace in every taut inch of him. "I don't want to be let off the hook. I want nothing more than to learn that you are carrying my child."

Her heartbeat drummed in her ears. Here was the edge she'd sensed before, a vast drop-off into the unknown. She longed with all her being to step back from it. And couldn't. "And if I am?" she whispered.

Anger leaped to life in those blue eyes. "You won't be handling it on your own," he said softly. "Especially if, by 'handling it,' you mean to do away with my child."

"No!" She put out a hand, appalled. "Oh, no, I didn't mean that. I just—" She stopped and blinked rapidly. Oh, damn, her feelings were all over the place. She did not want to cry in front of this man. "I didn't how you felt, or if you wanted a child, or..." Or if she would ever see him again. Or if she even wanted to.

He stared down at her. What moved behind his eyes she couldn't tell, but some strong emotion slid through him. At last he reached out with the hand that didn't hold the blue and yellow box, and startled her completely. He put his arm around her shoulders. There was something unpracticed about the gesture, as if he had no idea how to go about offering comfort. "It will be okay, Jane. I'll take care of you." Awkwardly, he hugged her shoulders.

The very stiffness of his one-armed embrace dissolved her. This was genuine. This was *real.* She sniffed once, then gave up the battle. When the tears started she grabbed hold of him while everything poured out—all the pent-up worries of the last three weeks—in between tears and hiccups.

"I didn't know," she said into his chest. "I didn't know anything—if I'd ever see you again, or if you—*hic*—would call. You didn't. I didn't really think you would, but then—*hic*—then I was late with my period. But I couldn't find out what that meant, not for two weeks, because all the—*hic*—tests say to wait that long, so I tried not to think about it. And then, just as the two weeks were over, you showed up! And I *still* don't know anything!"

Samuel stood very still. "I don't—" He stopped. A heartbeat's worth of silence fell, then another. She hiccuped. He asked cautiously, "Do you need a drink of water?"

Jane closed her eyes. She poured her heart out to him, and he offered her a drink of water? She sniffed back the last of her tears, and pulled away. "Excuse me," she said stiffly. "I always get the hiccups when I cry." She headed for the bathroom for some tissue.

He followed. "Did you cry because of me?" he asked, standing in the doorway while she yanked a tissue from the box. "Or because you're afraid of being pregnant?"

For a man who never gave anything away about himself, he did like to ask impossible questions, didn't he? Jane glared at him and blew her nose. "I'd like that drink of—*hic*—water now, if you don't mind."

He nodded. "I'll get it." He held out the blue and yellow box.

Jane stared at it. There comes a time, she thought, when the most ardent coward can no longer avoid the facts. She took the box from him.

While he was gone, she opened it and quickly scanned the directions. When he returned and handed her a glass of water, she took it, then closed the door on him.

Several minutes later Jane opened the door again. Her hands were shaking. Her legs didn't feel entirely steady, either, when she walked the short distance to the living room, where Samuel waited by the window. But she wasn't hiccuping anymore, and her tears were gone.

He turned to look at her.

Jane licked her lips. The edge she'd feared was behind her now, and she was plummeting into the unknown, falling faster and faster. Fear and wonder kept her voice to a whisper. "According to that kit, I'm going to have a baby."

A smile spread across his face. A real smile. He wasn't pretending to be anything now. His joy at learning he was going to be a father was as honest and absolute as daybreak. Jane looked at the happiness on his face and finished her fall, and she never even noticed.

She was going to have a baby. *His* baby. The feelings that flooded Samuel were hard and clean and jubilant—as far removed from the shadows he'd lived in as the sun was removed from Pluto's lonely orbit. They overwhelmed him. In that moment he knew he wanted that baby with everything in him, and not just because it would bind Jane to him. Not just because it would make his plans come true.

Yet his plans *were* coming true, and it made Samuel want to sing and shout, only he didn't know how. Even before he'd joined the agency—long before—silence had meant safety. It took him a moment just to find words. "We need to celebrate."

She looked dazed. "I suppose…if I *am* pregnant, I shouldn't have anything alcoholic."

"'If'?" He looked at her sharply. "What do you mean?"

She tried a smile, but it wobbled. "I don't *feel* pregnant. But I guess that's silly. I don't have to feel it for it to be true, do I?"

Jane obviously wasn't as happy about this as he was. That realization hit him hard. It felt wrong. He wanted her to share his elation. He needed her to share it.

Samuel spoke four languages and understood two more. He had a near-eidetic memory and could break into a locked room or a password-protected computer with equal ease. He knew seven quick ways to disable a man, and fourteen ways to kill one. But he had no idea how to make a woman be happy that she was having his baby. He walked slowly over to her. "Why aren't you happy?"

"Why do you think?" Her smile slipped away entirely. "I'm pregnant, I'm not married, and I'm scared."

He could do something, then, to make her feel better. He'd intended to do it anyway. Relief was almost as large and overwhelming as the jubilation had been. "You'll be a good mother."

Her voice was tight and small. "A minute ago you were afraid I might get an abortion."

"I was wrong." He was sure of that. He'd allowed fear to edge out reason, but his fear had been foolish. A woman who rescued a beetle because she felt responsible for it could be trusted with a baby. His baby. "I meant what I said earlier, Jane. I'll take care of you."

"Well. That's good." Her eyes had an inward, anxious look, as if she were looking over her fears and stacking them up. "A lot of women in my position don't have that kind of support from their—from the father. I'll work this out. I'll get my feet under me again, and figure out what I need to do. My mother—'' That thought brought her to a stop. She shook her head. "I'll think about what to tell my mother later.''

"You could tell her we're getting married.''

"You already told her that," she said dryly.

"No. *You* could tell her. It could be the truth, Jane. If you want it to be.''

Her lip quivered, and her eyes got damp.

Samuel wanted to kick himself. He'd bungled it. He hadn't meant to say anything so soon. Hadn't she just accused him of pushing her? She wasn't ready to be persuaded into marriage. When she blinked rapidly, he felt a touch of panic. "Don't cry," he ordered her. Her tears had undone something inside him, tugging at a place he didn't want touched.

"Okay," she said. The smile she gave him then was slow and achingly sweet. "You want to do the right thing."

"Yes." He inhaled deeply. Thank God she understood. He wasn't sure what the "right" thing was, here in Atherton. The standards he'd lived by for years didn't perfectly apply, and he couldn't rely on his instincts. No one was trying to kill him. No nations would rise or fall, depending on what he did. But a gentle woman might cry.

Surely, though, it was right to marry the mother of his child. "I want to marry you," he said so that she would understand clearly.

"Did you mean it when you said you were going to stay here, then? Or were you thinking of some sort of a—a marriage in name only, so you could still go off and do your spy stuff, while I—''

"*No.*" He must have spoken too harshly, because her eyes got big and startled. "I told you, I'm retired. I want to live here. With you." He was close, so close, to having what he wanted. He could sense that. Why was he going about this so poorly? He made his voice and face soften. "I want *you*, Jane," he said, and reached both hands up to stroke her hair.

She liked being petted. He could see that. Her eyes didn't

shut, but they grew hazy with pleasure. So he kept touching her as he moved closer, watching her face to see her reaction.

She was soft, wonderfully soft. Her hair was cool silk, and her skin was warm with life. His hands drifted along her cheeks, her jaw, and down. He felt her nervous swallow in the smooth column of her throat, and the way her heart speeded up. Just as his had. "Jane," he said, and without stopping to consider the consequences, he bent and kissed her.

From one second to the next, everything changed. Her body was soft and welcoming. She smelled like lavender and rain, and he wanted her. He wanted her too much. He forgot to be gentle, to seduce. He knew only the fire in his blood, and his need for her.

He cupped her bottom in his two hands and pulled her to him tightly. The fire licked higher, burning away thought and doubt, the past and the future. There was only now. He groaned, and stabbed his tongue into her mouth over and over, mimicking the way he wanted to enter her body. And she wanted him, too. Her hands were eager on him, testing the muscles in his shoulders, his back.

And then they were pushing at his chest. For a moment he didn't understand what was happening—that she was turning her head away. Rejecting him.

A few seconds too late, he released her.

His breath heaved, hot and passionate, in his chest. She stared up at him, her eyes as wild as his, but he saw fear there as well as passion. "Samuel," she said, and her voice broke. "Samuel, I have to know if you—if you care for me."

He could have her. He knew it. The right words, soft words, and she would ask him into her bedroom, her body and her life. He could have everything he wanted—if he were willing to lie to get it.

He was very used to lying.

In the next few seconds, Samuel fought one of the hardest battles of his life. He had promised. He'd sworn to himself that he wouldn't lie to this woman, but that promise seemed small and unimportant in the face of the need sleeting through him. But faintly and from far off, he remembered what Jack had once told him. Jack, who had died because he'd come back for Samuel, just as he had promised he would when they'd had to split up on their last mission together. *"I don't make promises often,"* Jack had said in a sunnier moment years ago, long before Samuel had put on his current name. *"Only the ones I'm willing to back up, no matter what."*

No matter what. Samuel's muscles locked tight with the battle between need and necessity. "I'm sorry."

Hurt broke open in her eyes. Her arms fell to her sides, and she stepped back.

He fumbled for words. "I'm not..." Normal, he thought. "Not like the men you're used to. I can't feel what you want me to feel. But I do want you, Jane." Too much. He lost control with her. He didn't know what to do, how to take that hurt out of her eyes, or how to fix himself so he wouldn't lose it every time he kissed her. "I don't know what to tell you."

"You've said enough." She drew in a deep, shaky breath and turned away, hugging her arms around herself.

"You haven't answered me. About marriage."

"I'm going to need some time." She didn't look at him. "I have a lot to think about."

She said she needed time, but she responded to him as if tomorrow were no more than a myth. And he...he lost it. Every time he kissed Jane, he lost control. "Dammit to hell." He ran a hand over the top of his head, angry with both of them. He crossed to the couch and picked up her coat where she'd tossed it. "All right. Let's get out of here."

She did look at him then—one long, wholly dubious glance, as if he'd asked her to perform some unnatural act.

He couldn't manage a reassuring smile, not with the volatile mix of emotions still churning inside him, but he did keep his movements slow and nonthreatening. He took her arm. "I still want to celebrate. Come with me. We'll take my car." Her little compact didn't have enough horsepower to evade a charging Chihuahua. Samuel didn't expect to need to evade anything, but he wanted to know he could if he had to.

"It's too early for dinner," she protested weakly as he bundled her into her coat. "And I can't have alcohol."

"Chocolate sodas," he said as he hustled her out the door. "We can have chocolate sodas at the soda fountain." He hadn't bungled things completely, he decided. She was willing to go with him. He kept one arm protectively around her on the stairs. No doubt she was perfectly capable of descending the stairs without his help, but he didn't want to take any chances. She was carrying a baby.

His baby.

His spirits had lifted by the time they got into the Jeep. Chocolate sodas at an old-time soda fountain, he thought, and his face eased into a smile as he turned the key. It was the perfect way to celebrate his new, small-town life, and the new life Jane carried.

Eight

"**I** can't believe you brought me here," Jane said, resisting the urge to sink lower in her seat. The backs of the booths at Handy's Drugstore were high, but not high enough to hide behind.

"Why not? It's a great place." They were in the rear booth. Samuel sat across from her, with his back to the wall. He'd chosen that seat automatically, and his eyes scanned the room just as automatically every so often.

"I don't think you need to worry about terrorists," she said dryly. "Just keep an eye out for Liza. She'll be over, sooner or later, to see what she can pry out of us."

He smiled slightly. "We don't have to tell her anything."

"You don't know Liza. She could teach the FBI a thing or two about interrogation techniques." Because she needed something to do, she sucked at her straw. They did make a great chocolate soda at Handy's, and getting a little sugar into her system couldn't hurt. She was still shocky.

Not to mention pregnant. She sucked harder, but chocolate

wasn't enough. She couldn't shut anything out, nothing at all. Not the sight of that little test stick turning pink, or the look on his face when she'd told him. Not his stilted offer to marry her, or his kiss... That kiss. Just thinking about it made her warm in all the places he hadn't touched—places she'd wanted him to touch, and still did, heaven help her.

"Why didn't you want to come here?" he asked.

"About a hundred reasons. You can see one of them sitting up at the counter with his hamburger. That's Mr. Bryce, my Sunday-school teacher. And over at the register is Liza, of course—she's a very good reason. Then there's Raymond, the boy who just brought our sodas. He's in my fourth-period class." She could tell Samuel didn't understand. She shifted restlessly in her seat. She felt twitchy and angry and uncertain.

Also hot. Damn him. "Liza may already have mentioned the pregnancy test you bought to Raymond. She has no sense of discretion. If he knows, in a few days all my students will know."

"Will that create a problem for you, if your students know you're pregnant?"

"Yes!" She took a deep breath. "I might even lose my job. Did you do it this way on purpose, to put pressure on me?" It was going to be very hard to resist his offer of marriage once everyone from her former Sunday-school teacher to her students to her family was aware of her pregnancy.

"No." He paused before adding, "I might have, if I'd realized it would help me persuade you. I do want to marry you, Jane."

Her breath got caught in her chest. When he said things like that— No, she told herself firmly. No, she was not going to start thinking that maybe sex was a good enough reason to get married. Not even mind-boggling, ear-popping sex that flung her up and out, like a trapeze artist soaring without a net.

Without a net? Was she crazy? She was a woman who would always need a safety net. "We're not going to talk about that right now."

He gave her a level look that told her he could make her a lot dizzier, if he tried. But instead he sipped at his soda. Then his eyes did that check-out-the-room thing before he spoke again. "All right. What would you like to talk about?"

"Your retirement."

His eyebrows lifted. "I can't discuss my former occupation."

"Not that. I mean—you're not exactly retiring, are you? You're changing professions."

"You could put it that way."

"And you're really planning to settle here? In Atherton? Teaching history at the community college?"

He was quiet for a moment. "Do you find it so hard to imagine me teaching?"

"No," she said, surprising both of them. "Now that I think about it, you might be good at it. You've got the patience, and not much throws you. That counts for a lot when you're dealing with teenagers," she said dryly. "And people listen to you. Even when you're lying to them, they listen, as if whatever you say is sure to be important."

"I'm not lying to you."

She felt a flicker of something—there and gone too quickly for her to be sure what it was. Fear? Belief? She drew in a deep breath and forced her mind back to the subject. "What I find hard to imagine is you being happy to stay here in Atherton after the life you've led."

"Then you don't understand anything at all. Did you think I chose the work I did because I needed the excitement? Excitement junkies get killed. A lot of the time they get other people killed, too, and whatever situation they were supposed to deal with goes to hell in a handbasket."

"Then why did you do it?"

He shrugged. "I was good at it."

That was it? He'd done it because he was good at it? Jane worked at that snippet of an answer, looking for reasons. Maybe he meant that he had done the job because it had needed doing. Everyone needed to be needed, in one way or another. "How did you decide on Atherton?"

She could almost see him weighing his words, deciding how much to tell her. "When you met me, I had already decided to leave the agency. San Tomàs was my last job. Afterward..." His left hand lay on the table between them. He glanced at it, then began rhythmically opening and closing it. "I was in the hospital for a couple weeks, getting this taken care of. I had a lot of time to think."

"And you thought about...Atherton?"

He nodded. "The places I'd been before weren't right. They didn't have what I needed." Briefly, his gaze grew unfocused, as if he were consulting some inner vision. "I don't have a hometown. I want one."

He sounded determined. Not the least bit vulnerable. So why did his words make her want to put her arms around him and hold him close? This wasn't a man in search of comfort...but he was in search of a home. Jane couldn't help responding to the yearning she sensed. "Why don't you have a hometown? Did you move around a lot when you were little?"

"It's best if you learn the same things about me everyone else does. You aren't used to secrets."

"I want to know," she said stubbornly. "You asked me to marry you. If you're really someone else, not Samuel Charmaneaux, I deserve to know that."

He hesitated. "The man I used to be doesn't—"

"Hi, there, Jane!" said a brassy, cheerful voice right behind her. "When can I congratulate you two?"

Jane wanted to scream with frustration. Liza had found them. And soon after Liza came, so did Mr. Bryce, who stayed to chat after Liza had to go back to the register. After that, the mother of one of Jane's students stopped by.

They all wanted to know about Samuel. Jane didn't blame them for feeling the same pressing curiosity about the man that she did. She just wished they would all go away. He'd seemed on the brink of revealing something important, and now he was all closed up again—though she was probably the only one who noticed that. He was quietly charming to everyone, and gave every appearance of pleasure when someone new stopped to chat. In fact, he seemed to love it.

Because they were making him feel at home?

Jane watched Samuel with Mr. Bryce and contemplated the possibility that he *wasn't* acting. Not entirely, anyway. Something clicked into place for her, and, for the first time since Samuel had smiled at her in the bank parking lot, she knew what she was going to do.

Maybe she did have something he wanted. He hadn't been happy in his other life, the one he wouldn't talk about. Oh, he hadn't said so, but it seemed obvious to her from the few things he had said. He had come to Atherton because he wanted a hometown. Maybe he was hungry for connections—human connections, the kind that came from living in a small town where people knew you or at least knew who you were, the sort of place where the buildings had stories attached to them.

He was hungry for roots. For permanence. Hadn't he shown her that when his face had lit with joy at the idea of being a father?

She could give him those things. She could share her town and its history with him, as well as the baby they had made— the baby she didn't yet quite believe in. She could share her family with him. And if she gave him all of that, it just might be enough to make him stay.

Jane realized with sudden, dizzying certainty that she wanted very much for Samuel to stay.

Darkness was falling when Samuel slid behind the wheel of his Jeep. Jane hadn't wanted to eat at the drugstore. Nor had she suggested eating anywhere else. She seemed abstracted, and Samuel wondered if she was going to try to kick him out of her home again.

His jaw tightened. She was proving to be a lot slipperier than he'd anticipated, but he was flexible. And determined. "Your mother said your brothers and their families would be at dinner tomorrow night," he said, putting the Jeep into gear and pulling out into the street. "Should I worry about their reactions to our engagement?"

"Hmm? Oh!" She returned abruptly from wherever her thoughts had taken her. "Good grief, that is tomorrow, isn't it?

"Are they big, brawny types?" he asked lightly. "Should I worry about them catching me alone?"

"I don't think you have to worry about anyone smaller than Godzilla catching you alone," she said dryly. "And I can't picture them taking you out back to teach you a lesson, either. My brothers are rather overprotective, being so much older than me, but they're fairly nonviolent." She chuckled. "Except with each other."

"Tell me about them."

With a little prodding, he learned most of the facts he'd already read in the report, along with some new ones. Craig, her oldest brother, had married his high-school sweetheart, and he and Cherry had three children. When Jane was in high school, he had interrogated her dates. He thought of himself as the man of the family. She sounded fond and exasperated about that.

Bill hated vegetables and loved flying almost as much as he loved computers. Last year he'd married a lovely young woman, and they lived in Topeka with her two children from a previous marriage. His wife, Eve, was Jewish. Bill was considering converting.

Samuel had wondered, when he read about Jane's Jewish sister-in-law, how difficult it had been for the woman to fit into this small-town, Midwestern family. "How does your family feel about that?" he asked.

"Mama was pretty uncertain at first—right up until Craig got into the discussion. Craig argued religion with Bill until the two of them nearly came to blows."

He felt a sinking sensation. "That must have made her unhappy with her new daughter-in-law. She can't like having someone bring dissension into the family."

"Oh, no! It reassured her. Craig and Bill always argue. They *like* to argue. Good grief, they got into a fistfight over the last election. Mama has been breaking up their fights for too many years to be upset by that sort of thing, so when they got going over the question of Bill converting, that settled the issue for her. It became just another of those subjects her boys didn't agree about." She smiled. "Mama is a little fuzzy about some things, but she's as clear as can be when it comes to family."

Samuel couldn't think of anything more important than family, either. He silently approved of Marilee Smith's priorities.

They were coming up on the turnoff to Jane's street. "Last chance to change your mind about going out for supper," he said. "We're nearly home." He was surprised to hear himself refer to her apartment that way, but it felt good. It felt right.

"I don't want to eat out." She sounded tense again. "I've got some leftover chili I can defrost."

He wondered what the odds were of her offering him some of the chili before she tried to kick him out again. "Are you a good cook?"

"Yes." She tilted her head. "Are you fishing for an invitation to supper?"

"Yes."

"About tonight... You're assuming I'm going to let you stay with me, aren't you?"

"Hoping," he said smoothly.

"You certainly have very *active* hopes. They're a whole

lot like other people's plans. In any event, I've been thinking.''

Here it came. He pulled up in her driveway.

Her hands were clutching at each other in her lap. "You
want something from me."

He smiled as he turned off the engine. "Oh, yes." He was
imagining a few of the things he wanted when he turned to
look at her.

Her breath caught audibly. "I don't mean that. I mean—
what you *really* want. A hometown. You've picked Atherton
for some reason, and you want to fit in here. The easiest way
to do that is if you're associated with someone here—someone who knows a lot of people, who can help you make the
kind of connections you're looking for. That's why you were
asking all those questions about who I knew. That's why you
told people, right from the start, that we were engaged. Even
if we don't get married, you'll have a—a persona established
here. You'll be the man who used to be engaged to little Jane
Smith.''

He'd underestimated her. She had seen a great deal more
than he had realized. It gave Samuel an odd sensation to
realize she understood that much about him. "That's part of
it.''

"Well, that's the part I'm concerned with right now, because I can do that for you.'' She leaned toward him, her
expression earnest. "I can help you fit in here in Atherton.''

He was silent for a moment. "And what do you want in
return?''

"I don't— No, I guess I do want something. You were
right when you said it will be easier on me if everyone thinks
we're engaged. So I guess I want us to pretend to be engaged,
just like you first suggested. That's fair, isn't it?''

Samuel wasn't interested in being fair. He reached out and
cupped her cheek, leaning closer. "Aren't you forgetting
something?''

She didn't move. "Am I?''

He wasn't going to kiss her again. Every time his mouth met hers, something went wrong and he lost control. But he could touch her. He could feel the soft flush of arousal warming her skin, watch as it turned her eyes as hazy as the twilight falling around them. "I would rather our engagement wasn't a pretense."

"I—I know I haven't given you an answer."

"No, you haven't." He slid his hand down from her cheek and along the warm flesh underneath, then lower so that his fingertips could read the rapid pulse beating at the base of her throat.

"But for now, while I'm thinking things over, I... Samuel, I don't think you should be doing that right now."

"Don't you?" Her sweater was in the way, but for now he tolerated that, running his fingers through the hair at her nape instead of cupping her breast as he wanted to do. Her skin was cool there, chilled by the evening air. When the warmth of his palm penetrated, she shivered—which sent a thrill of excitement through him, an answering hunger that he restrained ruthlessly.

This wasn't the time to give in to his own needs. This time, *she* would need. He wanted her aroused and yielding, ready to say yes to whatever he asked. He lowered his head slowly, using the hand at her nape to tilt her face up to his.

She watched, her eyes huge and unblinking. "You want to stay here, with me. In my apartment."

"Yes." She wasn't retreating, wasn't refusing him this time, and the knowledge was heady. He wouldn't kiss her, he told himself, but surely he could skim his mouth along her cheek, sample the dusky flavor of her throat.

"All right," she whispered. "But on one condition."

He paused. His fingers tightened at her nape. "What?" She wasn't supposed to be thinking of conditions now, dammit. She wasn't supposed to be thinking at all.

"No kissing."

"What?" He raised his head, scowling down at her.

"While you're living with me," she said quickly. "I said I needed time to think, and I can't do that when you touch me. So while we're living together, I don't want you touching me and kissing me and—and all that."

Samuel didn't like it. He didn't like her stupid condition, or the fact that she'd been thinking straight enough to come up with one. He shook his head, trying to clear it. "You don't want me to kiss you or touch you while I'm living with you."

"That's right."

He pulled his hand back. It was easier to think when he wasn't touching her. After a moment, he smiled. It wasn't a particularly nice smile. "All right, Jane," he said softly. "I promise you I won't take advantage of our proximity in your apartment to touch you or kiss you. Is that what you want?"

She was frowning. Perhaps she sensed the trap hidden in his words. "I guess so."

"I realize you aren't sure you can trust me. After all, our only time together I wasn't exactly gentle with you, was I? To keep everything clear, if you change your mind about what you want, you have to tell me so. I won't set a foot in your bedroom until you invite me in."

"Well, I— There's the couch—"

"I won't take you on the couch, either." Though the idea was undeniably appealing. "Not unless you ask me to."

"That's not going to happen. Not unless..." Apparently she didn't want him to know what other conditions he was supposed to meet. She smiled tentatively. "I'm glad we got that settled."

Oh, so am I, Jane. Not that he was comfortable now, or sanguine about the direction she was forcing on his courtship. The next few days or weeks weren't going to be easy on him, but he had every intention of making sure they were even harder on her. That was the whole point of a seduction, wasn't it? Making sure she was the one who wanted the most. And the one who was willing to give up the most.

Nine

"**P**ass the potatoes, please."

"Mommy, Charlie's kicking me under the table."

"Am not."

"So, Samuel, what made you decide on Atherton?"

"Did you get any of the green beans, Jane?"

"Charlie, stop kicking your sister."

"Yes, I did, Mama. They're delicious."

"I didn't kick her. I barely touched her."

"Atherton has one thing no other place has," Samuel said, turning to look at Jane. He smiled.

She smiled back. She couldn't help it, even though she knew the intimate glance was part of his performance for her family. He looked so good to her. The dark navy of his shirt made the blue of his eyes deeper and more fascinating than ever—even if they were hidden behind those fake glasses.

So far, the meal was going well. There had only been one glass of spilled milk, and Samuel seemed to be dealing well with the usual mealtime chaos involved in putting seven adults and five children at the same table. She'd briefed him on what to expect. The moment they'd arrived, Jane had joined her mother and her sisters-in-law in putting the food on the table. The men were in charge of getting the children in place with hands washed and a minimum of fighting.

There was no dallying around with cocktails or appetizers at Marilee Smith's house. When you were invited to supper, you sat down and ate.

Jane glanced around the table. Her family might drive her crazy at times, but they were good people, she thought, her heart warming. Craig was eight years older than she was, a hearty, thickset man who might lack imagination, but he made up for it with his wholehearted devotion to his family. He sat at the foot of the table, reining in the high spirits of his eldest and helping Cherry keep an eye on the twins. He'd only spent the first ten minutes or so of the meal grilling Samuel about his professional prospects and financial status. For Craig, that showed great restraint.

Bill was the only one of them who resembled their father physically. Six years older than Jane, he was a wiry, dark-haired man who never sat still. His foot was undoubtedly tapping under the table right now. Anyone who didn't know better could easily have assumed that the redheaded boy sitting next to him had been born his son, based on their mutual fidgeting, rather than only having joined the Smith clan last year when Bill had married Eve, his mother.

Marriage could be a lovely way to grow a family, Jane thought. She glanced at the head of the table. Eve's children were one of the things her mother had loved right from the start about her new daughter-in-law. The more grandchildren, the better, as far as Marilee Smith was concerned.

Jane's hand went to her flat stomach. She'd worn one of her favorite dresses tonight, a teal-colored velvet that made her feel pretty. The material was soft and warm to the touch, but her hand was cold.

She hadn't been nauseous in three days. Not since Samuel had shown up. What did that mean?

Bill proved that his mind was, as usual, on computers, by breaking into the general conversation to ask Samuel, "What do you think about this new Internet bill they're trying to get through the House?"

"No politics at the supper table, Bill," Marilee Smith said firmly.

"Mama, it's not about politics, it's about computers."

"Not at the supper table. You can argue about it later, if you have to."

"Mommy!" came a shrill cry from the middle of the table. "Charlie's kicking me again!"

Jane glanced at Samuel. It occurred to her that a man who wasn't used to this much family could easily feel overwhelmed. Or he might feel left out, if he wasn't sure quite how to join in the chaos. She leaned closer to him and said softly, "You haven't cut and run. Does that mean you're enjoying yourself, or did the twins find Mama's superglue again?"

"'Again'?" He lifted his eyebrows, but there was a slight smile on his face. "I like your family, Jane. They're very lively."

"That's one way of putting it." Maybe, she thought, he really was enjoying himself. A person couldn't get much more connected than at one of her mother's family dinners.

"Your mother seems to be in her element."

Jane smiled. "Mama likes to say that she was put on this earth to spoil her grandchildren. There's nothing she likes better than having them around." She had two of them flanking her now—Benji and Anna, the two newest.

"Don't you think she'd like to know she'll be getting one more to spoil soon?" he asked softly.

Her heartbeat picked up. "Not yet, Samuel. I don't want to say anything until the doctor confirms it." She'd made the appointment that morning. The earliest opening she'd been able to get was next Friday—the afternoon of the day the Charity Ball took place. Jane licked her lips nervously.

"If Liza starts talking," he said quietly, "your mother might hear about it sooner than you'd like, anyway. Don't you think it's better for her to hear the news from us?"

"Not yet," she repeated. She wasn't sure why she was so insistent about waiting. Cowardice, probably. "I talked to Liza. She'll keep the news to herself long enough for me to know for sure."

His eyes held hers, steady and impossible to read behind those gold-framed glasses. "I wonder...." He glanced around. When he looked back at her, his voice held a hint of amusement. "I suppose that, while your mother might be delighted by the news, your brothers probably wouldn't be."

He was thinking of doing it, in spite of her wishes. She was suddenly sure of that. He was weighing the advantages of enlisting her family on his side by telling them about the baby against the disadvantages. And the only real disadvantage was the way she would feel if he did. Tension lumped in her throat, but he was looking at her so intently that a rush of longing got tangled up with heat and anxiety.

Jane had to look away. She jabbed at a couple of green beans with her fork. She didn't want to find out that her feelings were at the bottom of his list of priorities.

"I talked to Sandy Clemmons today," Marilee Smith said. "She has some kind of bee in her bonnet about you driving in with her to take one of those FEDA courses."

"That's FEMA, Mama. Federal Emergency Management Administration."

"Whatever. I know Sandy means well, but anyone with any sense can see that isn't your sort of thing."

Jane stirred her gravy into her mashed potatoes. "Actually, I was thinking about it."

"I don't know why," Craig said with brotherly bluntness. "It's a waste of time. You aren't exactly the calm, collected sort in a crisis."

Bill chuckled. "I'll say. Too squeamish. Remember how in high school Mama had to write her a note so she wouldn't have to cut up the frog in biology?"

"Cutting up a frog isn't exactly the same thing as coping with a disaster," Samuel said mildly. "Jane is quite capable of handling a crisis without falling apart. She does it all the time at school."

"Oh, well." Bill chuckled. "The sort of minor crises that a teacher deals with aren't exactly on a par with coping with the aftermath of a flood or a tornado."

"She coped pretty well with being chased by guerrillas, too." Samuel put the bite of roast into his mouth.

Jane was as taken aback as the rest of her family was by Samuel's unexpected defense. She didn't know what to say.

Her mother looked flustered. "Oh, but you wouldn't want to see her get involved in anything so dangerous. Rescue workers take such risks. When I think about everything that could go wrong, it makes my heart flutter."

"Why?" Samuel asked. "Being prepared for disaster is a great deal safer than being unprepared."

Craig had recovered from his surprise. "I don't imagine it matters," he said with hearty good humor. "She won't be having much time for that sort of thing, anyway, will she? Not if what I've been hearing about wedding bells is right." He beamed at them as benevolently as if he'd invented marriage. "Have you two set a date yet?"

Now was his chance. Jane's hand tightened on her fork. If Samuel wanted to bring up her pregnancy, this was the perfect time to do it. *We won't want to wait too long,* he could say, *under the circumstances....*

"Not yet," he said. "Jane and I are still talking out a lot of the details."

Her breath whooshed out.

"Oh, I hope you're going to have a big wedding!" Cherry exclaimed.

"Does this mean you've finally stopped saying you aren't

exactly engaged?'' Jane's mother asked, her faded eyes hopeful.

"Yes." Jane glanced at Samuel. His features were as elegant and impossible to read as always. "That's what it means."

"That's wonderful!" Eve said. "Listen, I know this little bridal shop in Kansas City where—"

"You will want all the frills, won't you, Jane?" Cherry asked.

"And my sister's friend owns it, so I'm sure I could get you a great price."

Anna's tiny voice piped up, "Grandma, I need to go wee-wee."

"Now, the Robinsons did lovely things with all those flowers at the VFW—"

"I need to go *now*."

"And there is more room there, but I love a church wedding."

Anna gave up on getting her grandmother's attention and turned to the other nearest grownup—Samuel. "Sam-you, will you take me to go wee-wee?"

"Of course," he said at once, and pushed back his chair. When he stood, the other conversations straggled to a halt. "I don't know where it is, however."

"Oh, dear," Jane's mother said, putting her napkin on the table. "I'll take her."

"I want Sam-you to take me." Anna spoke with the certainty of a not-quite-three-year-old who has her mind made up. She tilted her shiny dark head back to look up at Samuel. "You don't know where the bafroom is?"

"I'm afraid not," he said gravely.

"You gotta get me down first."

He held out his hands, she leaned into them, and he swung her down from the table to stand on her own two, tiny feet. She held up her hand. "C'mon," she said imperiously. "I'll show you where the bafroom is."

Samuel bent to take the little hand in his.

Eve pushed her chair back. "I can take her."

"Oh, sit, sit," Marilee said. "He's going to be family. He may as well have a turn at bathroom duty."

"Well…"

"What do you think about the Royals this year?" Craig asked Bill. "Think they have any chance of a pennant?"

As the mix of voices rose around her once more, Jane turned in her chair to watch as her niece led Samuel from the room. They made a heart-stopping picture—the tall, silent man walking so carefully beside the tiny dark-haired girl, listening as intently to her chatter as if she were confiding the world's wisdom instead of filling him in on her recent progress in potty training.

Jane watched as they turned the corner and headed down the hall. And still she sat, motionless, staring, her heart beating too hard and her breath caught in her chest.

"…do you think of lilacs, Jane? Jane!" her mother said.

She remembered how to breathe. "Oh…" Slowly she turned back around to face the others. "Lilacs. They're very pretty."

"They might be a little hard to find, though. It depends on when you have the wedding. Now, a fall wedding…"

"Mommy, Charlie's kicking me again."

The sound of her family's chatter washed over Jane, the noise blending into a background as familiar as the endless sighing of the prairie wind. She didn't hear what her mother thought about fall weddings, or her brothers' opinions on baseball, or whether anyone finally made Charlie stop kicking his sister. There was only room enough in her mind for the single, incredible revelation that had come to her when she'd seen Samuel with Anna.

This was one heck of a time for her to realize she was in love with the man. Or with one version of him—the one she *wanted* to be real.

The wind was up when they left. It caught at Jane's hair, blowing it in her face and making her clutch her jacket to her. She got into the Jeep before Samuel did. Craig was in his advice-giving mode, and had delayed his own family's departure so he could finish telling Samuel where and when. to buy a house in Atherton. The two men stood talking nearby.

She was in love. It was wonderful. And terrifying.

From the safety of darkness, she watched Samuel as he talked to Craig. He looked exotic to her, with his hair pulled back in a ponytail, as usual, and his long, dark coat flapping in the wind like the wings of some huge, predatory bird. His face was calm and closed as he gave her brother the same respectful attention he'd given little Anna.

He was a kind man, she thought. She suspected he didn't think of himself that way, but the quiet way he accepted others was a rare sort of kindness. Maybe one reason people listened to him was because he listened so carefully to them. Heaven knew she felt vital and important when he looked at her with that same grave attention.

She thought about what he had told her family—that she was capable of handling a crisis situation. Was that really how he saw her? As strong and competent?

Jane ached to know what he saw when he looked at her, but she was frightened of what she might learn. She was so terribly ordinary, while he— Well, whatever he thought of her, he didn't love her. That certainty lay heavily on her mind and her heart. But he wanted her. Or at least, she was pretty sure he did. He made her *feel* wanted, but his desire might be pretense—part of his design to acquire a home and family through her.

He hadn't been pretending on the island. He'd truly wanted her then, wanted her badly. She hugged that knowledge to herself.

At last her brother finished telling Samuel how to conduct

his business and headed for his car, and Samuel joined her in the Jeep.

"Craig means well," Jane said when Samuel closed the door. "He just has a way of making his advice sound like edicts."

"He seems to think I should buy a house," Samuel said. "In fact, he has one all picked out for me."

She chuckled. "That's Craig. He's that way with all the family. Handing out advice is his way of taking care of us."

His head turned toward her in a quick, startled movement. "I'm not family."

"But he's ready for you to be," she said gently. "Telling you what house to buy was how he let you know that."

Samuel didn't answer. She watched as he started the engine. His hands still fascinated her. Quickly, before she lost her nerve, she leaned over, the movement made awkward by the bucket seats, and kissed his cheek. Just as quickly, she sat back in her seat. "Thank you," she said softly.

"What was that for?"

"For telling everyone I'd be fine in a crisis. I suppose you were just saying that, but—"

"No." The light from the dash glinted off the frames of his glasses, but gave no clue to his expression. "I said it because it's true. I've seen you deal with a crisis, and you didn't fall apart. You might not have known exactly what to do, but that's what training is for. Are you interested in taking those courses your mother mentioned?"

"Well, I…yes," she admitted in a rush. "It's strange, since I'm not a person who copes well with risk, but I'd really like to."

"Then you should do it." He looked away at last and started to back out of the driveway. "Will you go walking with me?"

"'Walking'?" She shook her head, confused. "It's late."

"It isn't yet ten o'clock." She heard the smile in his voice, though it was too dark to see his face clearly. "The sidewalks haven't rolled up yet. I drove around town while you were at work today. There's a park not far from here. I'd like to walk there with you.''

The park on Second Street. She felt flushed and tender to think that he'd noticed and liked a place that was special to her. ''That's one of my favorite places.''

''Good. We can walk there, and you can tell me any stories you know about it. You can tell me about your father, too.'' He accelerated smoothly.

''My father? Why do you want to hear about him?''

''Because he's the reason you're convinced you can't take risks, isn't he?''

By day, Samuel had thought the park charming in its simplicity, a comfortable blend of old and new. The trees were old, mostly oaks and elms with a scattering of firs. Sidewalks wound in and out under their branches, directing visitors to swings or a sandbox, three different slides, brand-new climbing equipment, a picnic area or the gazebo at the center.

The park's character changed after dark. Night had a way of creating mysteries out of the mundane, he thought. Miniature streetlights imitating old-fashioned gas lamps illuminated the sidewalks, while the limbs of the trees clicked and shivered overhead, agitated by the wind. Away from the paths, the shadows were thick.

Atherton was as safe as any town could be, but Samuel remained very aware of shadows.

''We're not supposed to be here, you know,'' Jane said.

''Are we not?'' He looked at the woman walking at his side. Her cheeks were glowing, and her eyes gleamed with excitement.

She shook her head. ''Didn't you see the sign on the gate? The park is closed at this hour. It stays open late in the summer—that's why they put the lights in—but not in the winter.''

He'd seen the sign, and the wrought-iron fence that separated the park from the sidewalk. The fence, he thought, was more symbol than deterrent, since any halfway active five-year-old could climb it. But it was nice to know there were places where people respected the orderliness of fences.

At least, most of the time they did. He smiled at Jane, who was obviously taking great pleasure in defying this small rule. "Will we be arrested?"

She laughed. It went straight through him, that laugh, and he stopped walking to soak in the sound. He hadn't heard her laugh like that, free and all out, since they were on San Tomás.

She stopped, too, and tipped her head. "Is something wrong?"

"No." He wanted her to laugh again. "Why do they close the park at night? Muggers?"

"Oh, no." She seemed to find the idea amusing. "No, too many high-school kids think this is a great place to party. The town got tired of cleaning up the beer cans and passed an ordinance closing the park at night—earlier in the winter, later in the summer."

"And did that stop them from coming here to party?"

When she shook her head, the wind caught her hair and tossed it in her face. She pushed it back. "No, of course not. But they're a lot stealthier about it now. They don't have such large parties, so there are fewer beer cans. The city does patrol the place at night now, but in a hit-and-miss way. We're probably safe from arrest." She leaned closer, her voice dropping confidingly. "In the summer, the police patrol more often. The far side of the park ends at the creek, where there are lots of trees for privacy and enough grass to invite young couples to, uh, investigate nature."

He could imagine it—the quick, near-innocent fumblings in the grass, the stolen kisses and hasty couplings. "Nature is a wonderful thing." He reached out to finger the hair the wind insisted on blowing in her face. "You have such lovely hair," he murmured. "Did you 'investigate nature' here in the park when you were in high school?"

His fingers rested against her cheek, so he felt the sudden heat bloom there. "That's none of your business," she said primly.

He wanted to know, though. He wasn't jealous of whatever boy might have been the one to touch her first—not exactly. But he found he wanted to believe that unknown boy had been kind, and as gentle as any inflamed adolescent could be. He gave the strand of hair in his fingers a soft tug. "I think you did."

"For heaven's sake, Samuel." She was embarrassed, but her eyes still shone. She liked his teasing.

He smiled. "Just how naughty were you, down by the creek one warm summer night?"

"I'm not about to tell you something like that. Not unless you want to trade stories." Her smile said she was teasing him back. "Do you want to tell me about your first time?"

For a moment, he saw it again—the blanket tossed down on the grimy floor of a room at the back of an abandoned warehouse, the swing of shiny black hair against a girl's sallow face and her urgent, dark eyes. He remembered the sound of rats in the walls. She'd been seventeen and high, desperate for something he hadn't understood at the time, though he'd sensed even then that what she truly craved had little to do with sex. And he— Well, he had been handy, and much younger than she was.

But she'd shown him what to do, and at the end, she'd cried out his name.

Danny...

"Samuel?" Soft fingers stroked his cheek. "What's wrong?"

He shuddered. "Nothing," he said automatically. She was looking up at him, worry clouding her beautiful eyes. He managed a smoother tone. "I tell you what. I won't tease you about what you did down by the creek if you'll show me your *other* favorite thing to do in the park.''

She laughed again, and the sound reached deep inside him, brushing softly against his memory of the way a fourteen-year-old boy had lost part of his innocence. Her laughter made him feel clean inside, and young. ''So what will it be?'' he asked softly. ''The jungle gym, maybe?''

''Oh, no. I got stuck up there when I was five. I'm afraid of heights. I love to swing, though. And the most perfect swing set in the world is here in this park.''

Ten

He pushed her in the swing.

The stars were a soft glitter in the black of the sky, the wind was cold enough to sting as she flew up, up and out—then down again and backward, her hair rushing into her face. Her unbuttoned coat hung loose, and her velvet skirt flapped against her legs.

She loved it all—the sky, the wind…the man. "Higher!" she called out.

"I thought you were afraid of heights." He gave her another, harder push.

"Only when I'm standing!" The chains creaked as she soared higher, pumping with her legs. "I can be as risky as I like when I'm sitting down."

"Strange that the daughter of a tightrope walker would have that problem."

Wasn't it, though? Some of the joy went out of her flight. She leaned back, flowing with the motion as the swing descended from the heights. And she didn't answer.

His hands met her back. And pushed. "Have you always been afraid of heights? Or of risks?"

She closed her eyes, but that just made her dizzier as the swing climbed its predetermined arc. "I don't know. What does it matter? Papa didn't mind. He wasn't upset that I wasn't like him." She started back down.

"But you were." The push he gave was much gentler this time. "How old were you when your parents divorced?"

"Wait a minute." Her eyes came open, and this time when she swung back down, she dragged her feet in the well-worn trough in the dirt beneath the swing, bringing it to a twisting stop. She turned to look at him. "How did you know my parents were divorced? I didn't tell you that." She searched her memory. No, she'd mentioned that her father had died when she was young, but that was all.

His expression was curiously blank. "The agency I used to work for has access to background checks such as the one that was conducted on your brother. I read that report before I came here."

She remembered Bill mentioning casually when he took the government position a couple of years ago that it had involved a security check. Her eyes widened. "Did you check up on me?"

"If I hadn't, the agency would have after I became involved with you."

"You mentioned census data," she said slowly. "That first night, when you were asking me all those questions about Atherton, you talked about what the census data revealed. My God. Did you have the entire town investigated?"

He was amused. "It would be beyond the resources of my former employers to investigate the population of an entire town, I'm afraid. I got most of the facts about Atherton off the Internet."

She stood suddenly. She had let herself get entirely too dizzy.

"I wanted to know everything I could about you, Jane. Some women might find that flattering."

She moved away, hugging her coat to her, stopping at the edge of the shadows to turn and face him. The wind no longer felt exhilarating. Now it was only cold. "But were you interested in me? Or in what you could get me to do?"

He followed her. "You're avoiding the subject."

"The subject is a report on me and my family that's on record in some hush-hush agency you won't tell me anything about, and I'm not the one avoiding it."

He shook his head. "No, the subject is you, and when you developed this idea that you aren't a risk taker. You don't seem to want to discuss that."

She waved it away. "It's not important."

"Of course it is. You avoid risks because you don't think you can handle them. And you see me as a risk, don't you?" He stood too close again. Damn him, why did he keep doing that? He reached out and gently moved her hands out of his way, then slid his own hands inside her coat, circling her waist. His hands were wonderfully warm. His eyes were bright and unreadable. "Your brothers like thinking of you as helpless. Your mother sees danger in the simplest things. That should be enough to explain your doubts about your competency, but I keep thinking your father is involved somehow."

"There's no mystery to it. I'm just not very brave—though I've sometimes thought that if I'd been allowed to go with my father…"

"What do you mean?"

"At first, Mama went with Papa. Every summer when the circus went on tour, she and the boys traveled with him. Can you picture my mother living in the chaos and confusion of a touring circus?"

"No, I can't." He urged her closer.

With a sigh, she let him pull her to him. It was safe enough. He'd promised, and she believed he honored his promises. She did put her hands between them, though, resting them on his chest, trying to hang on to a little distance.

Or maybe she just craved the feel of him.

"How long did your mother travel with your father?"

"Until I was born. By then, she was ready to quit. Mama says it was too hard to take a baby on the road, but I think I was just an excuse for her to stop doing something she hated. Anyway," she said, her fingers spreading out on his chest, "after I came along, she didn't go with Papa anymore. They lived together while he was in winter quarters, but every summer we came to Atherton, where she was born. I was supposed to get to go with him for a few weeks when I was old enough—my brothers did, and Papa had said I could— but somehow it never happened. And then, after the divorce..." She sighed. "None of us got to go with Papa after that."

"So you never were able to be part of your father's life with the circus."

"No." The memories weren't hurtful, not after all this time, but they were bittersweet. "I got to see him perform, of course. Mama took us whenever the circus was close enough. I'll never forget how he looked, up there in the lights, balanced on that high wire...." She shook her head, forcing herself back down to earth. "It isn't really a wire, you know."

"No?"

"It's a cable about an inch thick. But that's still very slim," she added quickly, not wanting him to think that her father had lacked one ounce of daring.

"It certainly is." His hands shifted, moving up her sides a few inches, then back down in a gentle, soothing caress that somehow didn't soothe her at all. "Did your father come from a circus family?"

She no longer noticed the wind. "Heavens, no. He came from Middleton—that's about seventy miles from here. I've still got cousins there, but Grandma and Grandpa Smith retired to Florida a few years ago.'' She tilted her head. ''That's why I think I could have learned to be daring, if I'd just been able to travel with him sometimes.''

He smiled. ''Because he came from Middleton?''

''It wasn't bred in him, you see. The courage it took to walk that wire wasn't something he inherited. In fact, his parents were appalled when he chose a life with the circus. But he used to say it was all he'd ever wanted to do.''

''It must have been hard for him. Not being born into a circus family, he didn't acquire the early training he might have had. He mustn't have had the contacts, either, or the trust of circus people.'' One of Samuel's hands left her waist for her hair. He stroked it once, then threaded his fingers through it.

''Yes, it—it was hard. He worked as a roustabout at first. It took him several years to work into having his own act.''

He used his light grip on her hair to tip her head back. He's going to kiss me, she thought, and her lips parted involuntarily while her heartbeat went crazy.

But he only looked down into her eyes, his own heavy-lidded. ''Perhaps he only took those risks that came naturally, the ones that were necessary. The ones that were part of something he wanted very badly.'' His other hand left her waist, but not her body. It slid around to her stomach, and up. ''You might find you're every bit as much of a risk taker as he was, Jane—when there's something you want badly enough.'' His hand covered her breast firmly.

''Samuel!'' She was shocked, hurt…thrilled. ''You said you wouldn't— You promised!''

''In your apartment, Jane.'' He kneaded her breast, his long, clever fingers sending heat spiraling through her. ''I said I wouldn't take advantage of our proximity in your apartment to seduce you.'' He smiled. ''We're not in your apartment now.''

Jane knew she was insane to stand there and let him touch her this way. The man had deliberately misled her. She couldn't want his touch when he'd just proven how little she could trust him, could she?

But she did. She wanted this, and more. The sight of his face, tight with hunger, his eyes on hers while he deliberately aroused her, was unbearably exciting.

He bent, but still he didn't kiss her. He nuzzled her hair aside to whisper in her ear, "My promise doesn't keep me from touching you here." His thumb flicked her nipple, creating a small shock wave through the velvet that lay between them. "And now." He pressed a kiss to the skin just below her ear, then caught the same spot between his teeth and bit gently.

She gasped at the sweet surge of feeling. "Samuel…"

His fingers tightened on her breast. He lifted his head. His face was hard, his eyes shadowed. "I can be gentle. You don't have to be afraid of me. But we need darkness."

"What—?"

He answered her without words, his arms going around her to press her back, urging her into the deep pool of shadow beneath the nearest tree. It was very dark there, and she stumbled. Then her back came up against the solid girth of the trunk, stopping her.

He didn't stop. "Pretty Jane," he murmured, bending to press his face against her hair. "You smell so sweet." He pushed her coat open, and this time both of his hands claimed her breasts.

And, heaven help her, she let him. She ached for him to do everything he was doing, and more. Her back arched, pressing her breasts more firmly into his palms.

He groaned and went still. Then he reached down, down, and began gathering the skirt of her dress.

"No—not here—"

"I'm just going to touch you," he whispered. "Let me make you feel good, my lovely Jane. You know how good I can make you feel."

Oh, she knew. However much she'd tried to forget, she

hadn't. His hand stroked up her thigh, and she regretted, fiercely, the sensible panty hose she'd worn. She wanted to feel his hand on her bare skin.

And then his hand reached its goal, and she stopped thinking altogether.

"That's it, sweetheart," he said, his voice harsher than a whisper, softer than the night. "Open your legs for me. Yes, like that."

Helpless, heedless, she obeyed him, and he rubbed her there where she ached for him, there where she needed him. His fingers were slow and intimate and thorough, while his other hand continued to knead her breast and his mouth pressed kisses to her forehead, her cheeks.

And all at once it was too much. She couldn't just stand there and let him touch her. She had to touch him, too. Her hands went to his hair, but it was pulled back, as always, in that neat ponytail, and she gave a low moan of frustration. She wanted it loose, dammit. Even when he'd been deep inside her, his hair had been pulled back. She wanted to wrap it around her, to bury her hands in it when he kissed her. She tugged at it.

"What is it?" he whispered against her forehead.

"I want your hair loose. I've never seen it loose," she said, fierce in her need. "And I want you to kiss me."

He lifted his head. She could see nothing of his expression in the darkness, but she felt the tremor that passed through him. "Ask me into your bedroom, Jane," he said hoarsely. His fingers moved, doing something she could have sworn was impossible with her panty hose in the way. "Tell me you want me. Ask me to come to your bed, and I'll kiss you."

A twig snapped.

He moved so quickly! One moment he was leaning over her, his hands and his words equally intimate. The next he'd whirled, putting himself between her and whatever was out there.

"All right, now," a deep, vaguely familiar voice said from ten or twenty feet away. "I know you're around here somewhere. Saw your car parked right by the gate. Save us all some trouble and come on out."

Jane couldn't see a thing with Samuel's back pressing her up against the tree, but that voice... She knew that voice. Then the tautness went out of Samuel. A second later, Jane's memory connected the voice to her everyday life.

Sergeant Bob Brown of the Atherton Police Department had found them.

It was dark inside the Jeep, and far too silent. The quiet throb of the jazz ensemble coming from the stereo speakers only accentuated that silence. Jane hadn't spoken since the officer handed them each a ticket, but she kept shifting restlessly in her seat.

For once in his life, Samuel hated silence. "He didn't see anything, Jane."

"He knew what we'd been doing, though." The quiet rustle of clothing told him she'd shifted again.

Dammit, he wished she would sit still. He knew why she was so restless, and it was playing hell with his control. She'd very nearly wrenched that control from him already tonight. Jane, sweet and yielding to his touch, had inflamed him. Jane issuing passionate demands had made him half crazy. If the officer hadn't interrupted them, in another moment he would have done what she'd asked and kissed her. And then he would have done what they both wanted—he would have taken her up against the trunk of that tree.

But then what? Having taken her, could he have kept her? He slid a glance over at her. She was biting her lip, looking worried and thoughtful.

No, if he'd taken her tonight she would have regretted it, and then she would have kicked him out. His hands tightened on the wheel. "The officer wasn't shocked."

"I know." She sounded unhappy. "He was amused. He

thought it was pretty funny for people our age to be making out in the park.''

"'Making out.'" Samuel smiled. "I hadn't thought of what happened between us in precisely those words."

"Did it happen *between* us, Samuel?"

"I don't know what you mean."

"You knew exactly what you were doing, while I... I think things were a little one-sided."

"No." His hands clenched harder—hard enough to make his wounded palm throb. He took it off the wheel and rested it in his lap. "Not one-sided, Jane."

"But deliberate?"

"If you want to know if I planned to seduce you, the answer is yes. I was doing my damnedest."

"Why?"

"That's a hell of a question." He turned onto her street. Almost home, he thought with relief. It was odd that he would feel so good about reaching her apartment when he couldn't touch her once they got there. He very much wanted to touch her again. Soon. The impatience and frustration tightening his body were another threat to his control and to his plans. They made him regret the promise he'd given her, and Samuel didn't like to waste energy on regrets.

But this woman was making him feel a great many things he wasn't used to.

When she shifted this time, it was to turn and face him. "All right, so you were hot, too," she said, her voice low and taut. "But I can't help thinking that whole seduction scene was part of some secret agenda of yours. You're always trying to figure out how to get me to do what you want, aren't you?"

"I wanted you to ask me into your bedroom," he growled. "That's not a secret."

She was silent for a second before asking in a rush, "What's your name?"

"What?" He glanced quickly at her, then back at the road. "You know my name."

"Your real name," she insisted. "The one you were born with."

He felt an aching sense of anxiety and, oddly enough, of loss. "It doesn't matter. That person doesn't exist anymore."

"Of course he does. Down inside you, deep inside, you're still whoever you've always been. Don't you see? I don't know where you really went to school or what your parents' names were or—or whether you liked spinach when you were a kid. You're asking me to trust you with everything I am, but you won't let me inside! You don't want me to see *you*— just this Samuel-person you've created!"

Fear bit him—real fear, deep and sharp as a knife to the gut. He didn't know how to let her see him. He shook his head, trying to clear away the emotion, but it clung to him, clammy as a spiderweb, as he turned into her driveway. They were home. He took a deep breath, trying to relax his fear-tightened muscles, and faced her. "You don't understand. All the records of the name I was born under were destroyed when I joined the agency. That man truly doesn't exist anymore. I have to be Samuel. There's no one else for me to be."

She didn't say anything, and he waited with a peculiar twist of anxiety. He wanted her to understand. He *needed* her to understand, yet he didn't understand himself what was happening to him.

Finally, wordlessly, she answered. She reached out and touched his cheek—a single, light caress that told him nothing, yet miraculously soothed the feelings knotted up inside him.

He didn't speak, either, as he got out of the Jeep and went up the stairs with her to where a light glowed on her landing. *At least she hasn't kicked me out,* he thought as she used her key to let them both in. But it was obvious that Jane wouldn't be inviting him into her bedroom tonight.

Jane woke early the next morning, in spite of having lain awake far too late last night, keenly aware of the man sharing her apartment. Her apartment, but not her bed. It would have been so easy to get up, cross the hall and say his name. She'd been sure that was all she would have had to do—just speak his name—and he would have come to her.

She still wasn't sure why she hadn't.

The early-morning sun was soft at her window as she blinked herself awake. She thought about lying there awhile longer. Maybe another hour. Maybe a month or two. Avoiding Samuel sounded like a great idea, but it would be cowardly, wouldn't it?

If she were ever to acquire any courage, she had to start practicing.

Samuel was sitting on the couch, tying his shoes, when she came into the living room. The quilt he'd slept beneath was neatly folded across the back of the couch. He was wearing sweats again.

Jane was wearing her pink flannel nightgown with the powder-blue chenille robe her mother had given her for Christmas. She probably looked like a fuzzy Easter egg, but at least she was covered. She cleared her throat. "Good morning. I, uh, thought you might have slept in. Do you always get up early?"

"Usually." He finished tying the shoe and stood, his eyes on hers. "I like to run in the mornings."

She smiled hesitantly. "I'm sort of a morning person myself, once I've had my coffee."

"I made a pot. It should be ready by now."

"Oh, good. Thanks." Jane was glad she'd decided to be brave this morning, but she had no idea what to say next. "I guess I'll get a cup." She started for the kitchen.

"Jane…"

She turned.

His eyes searched her face. "I've always liked running. I ran track back in high school, until my senior year. Things were confused that year. I was in three different homes, in three different parts of the city.''

Her heart started jumping around in her chest like a nervous jackrabbit. ''Three different homes?''

''Foster homes.'' He paused. ''You can't mention that to anyone. That's not part of my official background. Not part of...Samuel Charmaneaux.''

Her jumpy heart took a sudden leap, and went soaring. He had told her something *real*. Something important. But her hands were less sure than her heart, and fiddled uncertainly with the tie that belted her robe. ''Were you in a lot of foster homes?''

''I grew up in them, off and on.'' He was entirely motionless now—even his eyes, which were fixed on hers. There was no expression at all on his face.

''I see.'' What she saw—what she could guess, from the little he'd said—was bleak. The usual reasons for a child to grow up in foster homes ''off and on'' involved abuse or neglect. Instinct told her not to press for more. She swallowed and asked as lightly as she could, ''So...did you like spinach?''

She could tell the moment he remembered what she'd said last night, because he relaxed. Humor gleamed in his eyes. ''I have *never* liked spinach.''

Jane grinned, giddy. ''Me, neither.'' Her hands dropped away from the tie at her waist. ''What are your plans for today, after your run?''

''I thought I'd fix Frances Ann's back door. Maybe she won't worry about prowlers so much if she has a decent lock. What did you want to do?''

''Work in the garden awhile.'' She'd felt a great many things around this man, Jane reflected. How odd that she would only now feel shy. ''I usually help Frances Ann with it because her arthritis won't let her do some things. I have to attend a meeting of the Combined Charities Committee this afternoon at two, but other than that, I don't have any plans."

"We'll come up with something." He started to leave, but paused at the door. "I'll see you when I get back, then."

"I'll be here."

He nodded once, as if she'd confirmed something important. Then he left.

Jane loved to grub in the dirt. It was usually good for whatever ailed her, and she had a lot ailing her today. Hope and indecision warred within her, and her stomach hurt. It wasn't the nausea she'd experienced off and on before, but a low, grinding ache that she put down to stress.

Turning over the soil, getting it ready for the bulbs she would buy later that day, was soothing. And while she worked in the dirt out front, Samuel was at the back of the house replacing the lock, and Frances Ann was in her kitchen baking them a big batch of caramel rolls for their help. It all felt terribly domestic, she thought as she dug the spade into the moist earth, and as seductive in its own way as his hands had been last night.

She could have this much. Whatever else he was or had been, he'd said he wanted to stay here and marry her, and she believed him. If she agreed, she could have a great many more mornings like this. Maybe building a home and a family together was enough. Maybe it shouldn't matter if he loved her or not.

She was grubby and slightly sweaty in spite of the chilly bite of early spring when a minivan pulled up at the curb a little after nine. Bill and Eve and the kids got out.

Jane stood, grateful for the interruption. Her thoughts and feelings were all over the place this morning. "Hi, there!" she called out. Benji, of course, reached her first. A four-year-old never, never walks when he can run.

"I want to dig, too!" he said, reaching for her trowel.

"I have a feeling your folks might not be too happy with

the results if you did," Jane said dryly. "Eve, I'd better not hug you. I'm grimy. I take it Mama persuaded you to spend the night with her before driving back?"

Bill shook his head. "You'd think we lived hundreds of miles away, the way she worries about us being on the road at night."

"I suspect she just wanted an excuse to keep the kids around awhile longer," Eve said. She stood with one arm linked with Bill's, her other hand holding little Anna's. "We thought it would be nice to stop by for a cup of coffee before heading back, but if you're busy—"

"No, no." Jane pulled her gloves off. "I can finish up later. Come upstairs and I'll put a fresh pot on."

A small, distinct voice piped up. "I want Sam-you."

Eve made the usual parent noises about "not imposing."

"Nonsense. I'm sure he'd like to see Anna, and Benji, too. He's putting a new lock on Frances Ann's back door," Jane said cheerfully. "Benji, why don't you take your sister around back?"

"Maybe that's not a good idea," Bill said. "If Samuel isn't used to children, he won't realize how much watching this pair needs."

She thought about how aware Samuel was of his surroundings at all times, and of how quickly he'd responded to Anna's request last night to take her to the "bafroom." "You don't have to worry. He'll keep track of them."

"Listen, Jane, I'm going to be blunt. What do you really know about this man?"

Jane stiffened. "What is it you're implying?"

Bill ran a hand over the top of his head. "I just have some questions, that's all. You can't know very much about him, as fast as all this has happened."

Jane sighed. She really was not in the mood for this. Bill didn't hand out advice the way Craig did. He worried.

She had enough worrying her already.

"Uh-oh," Eve said. "Just remember, Bill—I warned you not to do this, and I have no qualms about saying 'I told you so.' Benji, Anna, come on. Let's go say hi to Sam-you."

Eleven

Samuel was crouched in the doorway, using a drill to put the last of the wood screws into the frame, when he glimpsed movement out of the corner of his eye. He twisted, still crouched, every sense alert—and had just enough warning to steady himself before Anna threw herself at him and flung both arms around his neck.

Her brother was right beside her, but Benji was more interested in the toolbox than in hugs. Samuel switched off the drill and took the hammer away from Benji. Anna was chattering a mile a minute about some robots she'd seen on TV. Benji wanted to know if he could use the drill.

It all felt sweetly, beautifully ordinary.

Frances Ann, who was only a few feet away in her kitchen, spoke before Samuel could. "Why don't you children come have one of these caramel rolls I just took out of the oven?" She wiped her hands on a dish towel, delight wrinkling her face into a well-mapped smile.

Samuel slid his arm around the little girl, lifting her with him as he stood. "Would those be my caramel rolls you're giving away? I don't know that I'm willing to part with any, after smelling them baking the past half hour."

"Are there any nuts in them?" Benji asked suspiciously.

"Hi," Eve said as she rounded the corner of the house. She was a small woman on the skinny side of slender, with large, dark eyes like her daughter's, and hair the same vehement red as her son's. "Sorry about the invasion. Benji, when someone offers you a treat you either say, 'Yes, thank you,' or 'No, thank you.' You don't interrogate them."

"I found Sam-you, Mommy," a clear voice piped up from near his ear.

"So you did, honey."

Within a few minutes it was established that the rolls did not have nuts, that Samuel could indeed spare a couple of them, and that the tiny elf in his arms wanted one, too. He set her down reluctantly. She was so small, so vulnerable. So trusting. And in a few months, he thought, he would have his own small being to protect. A strong, bright feeling filled him.

Frances Ann disappointed both children by telling them to come with her and wash up in the bathroom before eating.

"Looks like putting in a lock turned into a carpentry job," Eve said.

He went back to work. "The wood in the frame was old. There wasn't much point in installing a new lock when an intruder could splinter the frame with one good kick." A last buzz of the drill and he had the frame in place.

"Home repairs do have a way of escalating."

Home repairs. Samuel turned the phrase over in his mind and decided he liked it. He reached for the dead bolt he'd purchased yesterday. "Where's Bill?"

"Upstairs making his sister mad," she said cheerfully. "I told him not to interfere, but he's bent on being a big brother and passing out warnings."

"Oh?" His stomach clenched with sudden tension. Samuel

masked the reaction by concentrating on fitting the dead bolt into the hole he had cut earlier. "Does he not approve of my marrying his sister?" Much of the battle to winning Jane's hand lay with her family, he thought. They meant a lot to her.

"Oh, I don't think it's that, so much. Mostly he's afraid she's rushing things." She waved a hand. "He and I dated for over a year before we became engaged, but our situation was different. My first marriage had left me with some scars, and I was worried about marrying outside my faith. My family wasn't happy about the idea at first."

He fitted the first of the screws in place and picked up the screwdriver. "The Smiths seem to have welcomed you." He'd been very aware of that last night. It had given him hope. If they could accept a daughter-in-law with a background very different from theirs, they might be able to accept him, too. Not that they would ever know just how different his background was.

"They're wonderful people. All any of them really needed to know was that I loved Bill, and he loved me. You and Jane have that part down pat." She smiled. "Jane's not one to hide her feelings, is she? Every time she looks at you, it's obvious she's head over heels in love."

The screwdriver slipped, scraping skin on his left hand. He didn't notice. "I..." Jane was in love with him? No, he thought. No, Eve was seeing what she expected to see. People did that. Jane wanted him, that was all. Samuel didn't know much about love, but he understood wanting.

"Oh, dear. You hurt your hand."

"It's okay." But if Jane *were* in love with him, she would truly be his. She would give herself to him completely. The thought made him light-headed, as if he'd shot up all at once to some point beyond the clouds and all the shadows they cast. Yet, if she loved him, she would expect him to love her back.

Hope crashed, flattening his thoughts to a thin, formless

gray. He could give Jane a great deal, but he couldn't love her. He didn't even know what love was.

She shifted from one foot to the other. "I hope you didn't mind my speaking up."

"No." She had meant well. It wasn't her fault that what she'd intended as encouragement had the opposite effect. He made an effort, and smiled. "I appreciate the reassurance."

Frances Ann and the children came back then, amid plenty of noise. The older woman settled the children at the table with the warm rolls, then called out to see if Eve had changed her mind about having one.

"I could be talked into it. They do smell wonderful. That is, if their rightful owner can spare another one." She gave Samuel a teasing glance.

Samuel allowed that he probably could, as long as it was a *small* one. Frances Ann was so pleased by his greed that she promised to bake him another pan of caramel rolls if this one wasn't enough.

Eve paused on her way into the kitchen. "Marilee already adores you, and Jane's brothers will welcome you, too, once they see you're good for her—even that hardheaded one I'm married to." She shook her head ruefully. "When I left Bill, he was busy telling Jane she doesn't know enough about you. Isn't that silly? She knows what she needs to know. Love may not be all that matters, but it's the most important thing, isn't it?"

His hands were steady as he set the next screw in place. So was his voice. But it took tremendous effort to keep them that way. "Of course."

"You really need to get that hand cleaned up. It seems a little stiff."

His hand was stiff from a knife wound, not from a minor scrape with a screwdriver. He shifted his body slightly as he picked up another screw so she wouldn't get a good look at it. "I'll take care of it when I'm finished."

"I see. You'd rather wait and let Jane tend your owie."

She grinned. ''Bill loves it when I fuss over some little nick or scrape of his.''

Samuel thought of Jane's reaction when she'd first seen his wounded hand. This time, his smile came more easily. ''Jane does make a fuss when I'm clumsy with a tool.''

Carefully, he set in the last screw and began tightening it. He couldn't give Jane love, but he had given her a child. That would be enough, he told himself. It had to be enough.

Jane spent the rest of the day defying physics by being in two places at one time. On one level, she spent the day in the familiar streets and buildings of Atherton; on another level, she was in a state of confusion.

She and Samuel went to the nursery together to buy daffodil bulbs, then swung by a friend's house to borrow a chain saw. While Jane set out the bulbs, Samuel cut the dead limb off the tree out front. They took turns cleaning up, then ate a late lunch. And they talked. Or at least, she did. Samuel wanted to know everything about Atherton and what it had been like to grow up here, and if Jane yearned to believe he was as interested in her as he was in her hometown, she didn't know how to stop.

It didn't help that he kept touching her. Not when they were in her apartment—no, he'd kept his word about that, and it was entirely her own fault if she responded to those innocent touches. When he brushed the hair from her face because her own hands were grimy from planting bulbs, it shouldn't have made her pulse rocket in anticipation. When he took her hand at the nursery as they walked among rows of plants, it shouldn't have made her think about other places his hand might touch her.

Then, when he dropped her off at the bank for her meeting, he kissed her.

It was a light, undemanding kiss, over almost as soon as it began; exactly the sort of quick goodbye a man might give his fiancée. There was nothing exciting about such a perfunctory kiss, surely.

But when he pulled his head back—too quickly—he left his taste on her mouth. His hand lingered at the nape of her neck, his long fingers sending shivers through her. And his eyes burned like blue fire. "Have I told you how much I love your hair?" he murmured.

"N-no." When he looked at her like that, she believed all sorts of things. That he loved her hair. That his touches today hadn't been casual, hadn't been part of his performance as her fiancé. She believed he'd touched her because he couldn't keep from touching her. The idea left her breathless and very definitely excited. "It's pretty plain."

"'Pretty,' yes. But 'plain'?" He shook his head. "Your hair is like the rest of you. Soft to the touch, with fire hidden in its depths." His gaze drifted to her mouth. His fingers tightened on her neck.

She was sure he was going to kiss her again. Really kiss her.

Instead, he sat back abruptly. "I thought we might go to a movie after you finish here, then maybe out to supper."

Disappointment and hunger knotted together in her chest. "I…" She stopped to clear her throat. "What's playing?"

"Does it matter?" His smile was slow and full of shared secrets. "I hadn't planned to watch the movie, Jane. I thought we could sit in the back of the theater and make out."

Heaven help her, it sounded wonderful. She didn't know how she was going to sit still for the next two hours, thinking about it. About him. "I'm not going make a date to go make out." She reached for the handle to the door.

"We'll talk about it when I pick you up. You think you'll be finished about four o'clock?"

She nodded.

"I'll be here."

Jane, uncertain whether that was a promise or a threat—

or what the difference between them was anymore—left as quickly as she could.

The night was cold and clear and filled with stars. The darkened interior of the Jeep was filled with the plaintive throbbing of jazz. Jane leaned her head against the headrest and let the sexy rhythms wash through her.

They had driven to a nearby town for dinner—after spending two hours in the back of a darkened theater, making out like teenagers. Or almost like teenagers, she thought, turning her head to look at him. He had dressed for their date tonight in the dark colors he seemed to favor. His shirt was black and open at the neck, and the sport coat he wore over it was a tweedy blend of dark colors. Even his jeans were dark, a new, unfaded indigo.

At the theater, Samuel had nibbled on her neck and played with her hand. He had teased her by almost, but not quite, touching her in places a woman shouldn't be touched in public. They hadn't been truly in private, after all, though no one had been sitting nearby.

But he hadn't kissed her.

She ought to be glad of that, but she wasn't. She moved restlessly in her seat. They were nearing Atherton now, and once they reached her apartment…what would happen then? Nothing, she told herself, and sat up straighter. She just had to use a little willpower.

Making conversation might help. She could use a distraction. "I don't know much about jazz. Who are we listening to?"

"Chuck Mangione. It's an old recording, but one of my favorites. This particular song is called 'Lullabye.' Do you like it? Some people prefer music with vocals, but I like the instrumentals best."

"It's beautiful. Very moody and emotional." Which made this an odd choice in music for a man who valued cool control above all else, didn't it? She tipped her head to one side. "How did you get interested in jazz?"

"I worked my way through college. One of my jobs was in a jazz club, tending bar."

"Were you in a band?"

"No. I have a decent ear, but I never wanted to perform. Just to listen. Jazz is like—I don't know—like listening to the night or the wind or anything else that has a voice, but no words."

Was there a part of Samuel that lacked words? Feelings buried so deep they didn't even have a voice, and could only be heard through the wail of a sax? Jane swallowed and told herself she was being fanciful. "You haven't brought any of your CDs into the apartment, and you have quite a collection. Don't you want to listen to them?"

"I didn't want to be pushy. Most of the time, you've hardly been willing to let me stay."

She had to smile at his idea of what was pushy. "I don't mind if you listen to your music." Especially not when it meant so much to him. She thought about what he'd said about working his way through college. "Was that job in a jazz club part of your real background, or the public version?"

He gave her a quick, unreadable glance. They were in the outskirts of town now. "As much as possible, we made my new background agree with my original one."

What does that mean? she wondered, frustration edging in. That he had really worked in a jazz club? That he'd really gone to college? "So it's okay if I mention you working your way through college in a jazz club?"

He nodded.

"What college did you go to?"

"My records show that I attended Eugene Lang in New York," he said carefully. "It's a strong, though untraditional, liberal-arts college, an excellent place for someone interested in history. I did my graduate work in California, with the assistance of a scholarship.''

''Yes, and you can probably tell me what the student center there was like, and where you went for the holidays. You pay a great deal of attention to detail, but none of that is real, is it? Where did you really go?''

A muscle tightened in his cheek. ''I can't tell you that.''

''I don't see why not! Surely it can't be a breach of security for me to know where you really attended college.''

''This isn't a game, Jane.'' For the first time, she heard temper in his voice. ''I'm not going to risk my life in order to indulge your curiosity.''

His anger startled her, but it didn't stop her. ''How could that risk your life?''

''Because I have to *be* the man who graduated from Eugene Lang, not someone who doesn't exist anymore.''

''What is it you're afraid of? That someone from your former life could find you here and—well, come after you, or something? But even ex-CIA agents retire under their own names. Shoot, some of them have written books about it.''

''Dammit, Jane, drop it. This is something I know one hell of a lot more about than you ever will.''

She was acutely aware of that. They were so different. There was so much about him that remained beyond her grasp; so much he wouldn't—or couldn't—let her share. ''I don't know why you picked me when you decided to make yourself a new life. You could easily have found a woman who didn't know you'd ever been anything except a history professor. Someone who wouldn't ask any questions.''

''But you're the woman who is having my baby.''

Her throat tightened. That was why he wanted to marry her. Because of the baby. She knew that, and truly it was a good reason. An honorable reason. Still, it took a moment before she could speak. ''You didn't know about the baby when you came here.''

''Not for certain, no. There was a chance, however slim,

and I was willing to take it. Once I got here, I knew I wanted to stay.''

They had reached her house, she saw with dim surprise as he braked to turn into the driveway. ''Because you liked Atherton so much?''

''It's perfect.'' He cut off the engine and leaned his arms on the steering wheel, looking around as if he could see the town he wanted to claim as his own. ''The people, the buildings, the park we went to—I like everything about it.'' He glanced at her. ''I like your family, too, Jane. Your brothers argue, but it doesn't matter—not in any lasting sense—because they are family, and your mother never lets them lose track of that. I like your mother, too, and the way she dotes on her grandchildren, even the ones some people would say aren't really hers to dote on. And I think, given time, they'll accept me.''

Jane's heart turned over. He wanted that, she knew. He wanted a family as well as a hometown, and she could give him those things. All she had to do was marry him without knowing his real name. She spoke without thinking. ''They've already accepted you. I mean, they will if I—'' She barely stopped herself before agreeing to anything and everything he asked of her. ''It's late,'' she said. ''We'd better go in.''

She got out quickly, but she didn't move fast enough. He caught her arm before she reached the foot of the stairs.

Very little light from her porch light reached them there. His face was a pale blur in the darkness. He held on to her with both hands, as if he were afraid she might escape. ''I like your town and your family, Jane, but I *want* you. There's a difference.'' His hands moved on her arms in a slow caress. ''A big difference.''

He pulled her against him. His body was warm and solid, and they weren't in her apartment yet. Desire twisted inside her—a coil as wild and natural as the snake that had once traveled across their hands. Surely, she thought, I can handle this much. All she wanted was a few more moments to feel this heat stretching lazily in her belly, a few more moments to enjoy his warmth, maybe a good-night kiss.... That wasn't so much to risk.

When he bent his head, she was ready, her lips parted. But he didn't kiss her mouth. His lips skimmed her cheek instead.

Maybe he needed a little encouragement. She put her arms around his neck and pressed herself against him.

"Jane." His hands tightened on her arms. His voice deepened. "I won't be rough with you this time. Ask me in, Jane. I want to be invited into your bedroom and your bed tonight."

Maybe she'd offered too much encouragement. "You're going too fast for me," she said shakily.

"'Too fast'?" When he raised his head, his mouth was turned up in amusement, but his eyes had a harder glitter behind those lying gold glasses. "I'd say I've been pretty damned patient. You're pregnant with my baby. I already know how it feels to be inside you. I know what you look like when you climax."

She stared up at his beautiful, mysterious face, and all at once she didn't care about risks or consequences. She wanted to see the *other* man. The one who had made love to her on a forest floor. "Your name was John, then. And you weren't wearing *these*." She reached up and pulled off his glasses.

"What the hell—?"

"I don't want you wearing them when I kiss you," she said, and grabbed his head. It was awkward, because she held his glasses in one hand and he wasn't helping, damn him. He stood stiff and unmoving. But he wanted her. Even though for some stupid reason he was resisting her efforts to get his mouth on hers again, she knew he wanted her.

Slowly, his head began to descend. She stood on tiptoe, ready to meet him more than halfway. Then he stopped. He straightened, in spite of the way she was tugging on him. She made a frustrated sound. Then his muscles were fluid again, not stiff—but he was moving in response to his will, not hers. He lowered his head, but not for a kiss. His words reached her ear in whisper-soft puffs, just as they had on the island, when they'd been in danger. "Someone's here."

Her eyes went wide.

He grabbed her hand—the empty one—and pressed something hard and metallic into it. The keys. "Get in the Jeep and lock the doors," he said in that barely there voice. He grabbed his glasses from her other hand and slid them back on his face. And then he was gone.

She stared after him, blinking into the darkness. He had taken his glasses. He thought he'd seen or heard Frances Ann's prowler, and he'd put his glasses on before leaving her. That was all she could think of while she stood there, stupid and shocked by revelation.

What if the glasses weren't a lie? What if the quiet professor and the secret warrior were *both* true—both part of the same man?

Jane stood very still as realization crashed down on her. Maybe Samuel couldn't tell her about himself, but he'd been showing her. All along, he'd been showing her the man he was. She hadn't understood, hadn't trusted what she saw...or what she felt. But now she knew, with simple, soul-shattering certainty. The man she'd fallen in love with wasn't an illusion.

A loud thrashing through the bushes sounded from the front of the house. Fear jolted her out of her reverie, but it was too late to follow instructions and get into the Jeep. She heard running feet, headed toward her. No way was that noisy flight Samuel. Jane pressed herself up against the wall of the house where the shadows were thickest, trying to imitate Samuel's ability to disappear.

A second later she saw a dark figure running flat out across the front of the drive, where the house lights didn't reach. No, there were two dark shapes, one right behind the other. Then the two shadows were even with each other and the action dissolved in a blur, as the two figures first locked together, then suddenly separated when one fell to the ground.

"Samuel!" She ran forward.

"Dammit, I told you to get in the Jeep!"

The standing figure was Samuel. She couldn't see his face, but she knew the shape of him. She recognized his fluid grace when he knelt beside the man lying motionless on the cold concrete.

"There wasn't time," she said, stopping about five feet away from the sprawled feet of the intruder. "You caught him. Is he—?"

"He'll live," Samuel growled.

Frances Ann's porch light came on. When Samuel lifted his head to look at her, that light reflected briefly off his glasses. "Go tell Frances Ann to call the police. I've caught her prowler."

The police arrived quickly. That was another reason to live in a small town, Samuel thought as he watched the patrol car pull away from the curb with the would-be burglar in the back seat. The cops here weren't overwhelmed by the sheer number of crimes taking place. In fact, he'd had the impression that the attempted break-in was the most interesting thing those two officers had dealt with recently.

"Oh, my," Frances Ann's quavery voice said from behind him. "That was terribly exciting, wasn't it?"

He turned, smiling at the older woman reassuringly. Frances Ann in her night attire was quite a sight. Her robe was striped with garish bands of pink, purple and green, and her head had sprouted spongy pink curlers all over the place. "He won't be bothering you again."

"Oh, I know that!" She patted his arm. "You were splendid. Simply splendid."

He was glad someone thought so. Jane had acted damned odd ever since he'd taken down the intruder, giving him searching, sideways glances but not saying much of anything.

She'd escaped upstairs to her apartment as soon as the police had finished with her.

"The officers were so nice, so understanding." Frances Ann leaned forward confidingly. "I think they felt guilty. None of them really believed me all those times that I told them someone had been prowling around the house, but they do now, don't they?"

"Yes, ma'am." Samuel decided not to tell the older woman what he'd heard from one of the officers. The young man they'd arrested was a known drug-user with a B and E record who used a police scanner to help him plan break-ins. They suspected he'd noticed all those calls they'd had from Frances Ann and had decided they would be a little slower to respond on the tenth call than they'd been on the first two or three.

"Maybe you should go in now," he suggested. The burglar hadn't yet managed to break any locks when Samuel had heard him tapping at one of the front windows. "I know you're enjoying all this, but my nerves are shot, and I can't go collapse until you're out of sight."

She giggled like a girl. "How you do go on. I think you want to see how Jane is doing. She did seem a little shaken by all this."

"I think you're right."

Frances Ann allowed him to walk her to her door. As he took the stairs up to Jane's apartment, he wondered if "horrified" described Jane's reaction better than "shaken." She'd asked about the intruder right away, as if she'd thought Samuel might have casually killed the man instead of just knocking the breath out of him.

Of course, Samuel admitted grimly as he started up the stairs, Jane had reason to know he was capable of killing. Yet he found he was angry, and growing more so with every step. He didn't like the feeling. It seemed to come from nowhere, and that made him feel out of control. He paused on the landing, breathing deeply, trying to regain his usual calm.

It occurred to him that he would have to knock to get in. He didn't have a key.

Dammit to hell, why hadn't she at least given him a key? He pounded twice, hard, on her door.

"It's open," Jane called from the other side.

Open? He tried the knob and, sure enough, the door swung open. "What the hell do you think you're doing," he snarled as he entered, slamming the door behind him, "leaving your door unlocked? You just had ample evidence how unsafe that is!"

For some reason, she didn't have any lights on in the living room. The only light came from her bedroom. It fell softly on her where she stood near the couch. And she wasn't wearing her fuzzy robe. Tonight she had on satiny pajamas in a soft, pretty shade of green. As soon as he saw her in them, he stopped dead.

She lifted her eyebrows. "With two cops and you right outside, I didn't think locking the door was really an issue."

It was unfair—it was *damned* unfair—for her to prance around in those pajamas. The shiny material emphasized her rounded shape too enticingly, making shadow and light equally slippery on her curves. Hunger bit him hard. He managed, barely, not to go to her and show her how much of a fool she was for wearing green satin. "Where's your robe?" he demanded.

"In my bedroom." She frowned. "You're in a funny mood."

"You're the one who's acting funny," he muttered. There was music playing, he noticed—something soft by Debussy. It was coming from her sorry excuse for a stereo. For some reason, though, the sound was exceptionally clear and lovely tonight. He took a step forward. "If you want me to keep my promise, you'd better join your robe in your bedroom."

"I'm not worried about that," she said softly.

She ought to be. He'd moved several steps closer, and he

didn't even remember moving. "I didn't hurt the guy, you know."

"What? Oh, you mean the prowler. I know that." She took a deep breath, which did distracting things to the satin covering her breasts. "There's something I need to ask you. Something important."

Questions again. He felt a touch of desperation. She wanted to know too much.

"How much do you need your glasses?" she asked.

He ran a hand over the top of his head, puzzled beyond belief by what she considered important. She'd yanked his glasses off him before she'd kissed him, he remembered. "If you've got something against my glasses, I'll go back to wearing contacts."

She took a single, uncertain step toward him. "I don't dislike them. But you were wearing them the first time I saw you. On the bus. Then you got rid of them, and I thought— I thought they were fake, part of your disguise."

"They were." He shook his head. This was a bizarre conversation. "I'm slightly farsighted. I usually wore long-wearing contact lenses when I was on assignment. Having my glasses fog up or fall off at the wrong time could be worse than annoying."

Her smile trembled. "So on San Tomás you wore fake glasses over real contacts. But now you just wear glasses. Real ones."

He nodded. He had no idea what she was talking about, or why, but understanding began to seem unimportant. She was close enough now that he could smell the sunshine-and-flowers scent of the lotion she used. "Jane," he said hoarsely, "you really should go to your bedroom."

"Well…" The smooth column of her throat moved when she swallowed. "Actually, I didn't want to go in there alone."

His pulse pounded in his ears. "Are you afraid to be alone because of the prowler?"

"I am *trying* to ask you into my bedroom, but you are making it darned difficult!"

He couldn't speak. He tried, but he had no words. This time he had to get it right. He had to make sure everything was right for her. So, wordlessly, he took off his glasses and set them on the nearest table.

She looked at them, then at him, puzzled. Then she must have understood, because she took his hand, and led him to her bedroom.

Twelve

Jane's heart was pounding with mingled desire and nerves. She'd never seduced a man before. While Samuel had been busy with the policemen, she had taken a quick shower, rubbed on some lotion and pulled out her summer pajamas. It was the only nightwear she owned that was remotely seductive. Then she'd turned off all the lights except for the lamp on the table by her bed, and put on some music.

She hadn't been sure about the bed, though.

That morning she'd made it as usual, but when she'd walked into her bedroom after her shower, the tidiness had struck her as prim and uninviting. The whole bedroom was wrong for a seduction—sturdy, scuffed maple furniture, a cluttered dresser, eyelet lace comforter and ruffled pillows—but she couldn't redecorate tonight. So she'd messed up the covers, but that had been *too* messy. She'd tried halfway making it—pulling the covers up partway, then folding them down—but that had looked terribly obvious.

Jane had still been deliberating when Samuel's knock had

sounded on the front door. She'd assured herself that a man in the throes of lust wouldn't notice anything about the room, but now Samuel stood just inside her door, holding her hand tightly and looking around as if he were fascinated by her perfectly ordinary bedroom.

She obviously didn't know a thing about seducing a man. He was supposed to be looking at *her* that way.

He turned to her then, and his eyes were hot and tender and he raised his hands to cup her face. "Your room is like you. Soft and inviting, but durable. Built to last."

"'Durable'?" She grimaced. So much for her attempt at creating a romantic atmosphere. "Durable" women weren't the stuff of romance.

"I remember the way you crossed half a jungle without complaining, though your feet were bleeding." His thumbs stroked over her cheeks, sending little ribbons of heat shimmering through her. "You do what has to be done. I admire that. But I'd never known a woman could be so soft and so strong at the same time."

Soft and strong. Her lips lifted in a tentative smile. This was getting better. "I complained about the snake."

"So you did." He smiled back, but just with his mouth. His eyes were crowded with needs and shadows. "But not until it was safe. Like I said, you did what you had to do."

She thought of what had happened after the snake, after they'd both laughed like idiots. After he'd put his hands on her. She could tell he was thinking of that, too, from the sudden tension in his hands. He skimmed a kiss across her forehead. "I'll take very good care of you tonight, Jane. I'll make sure you don't regret changing your mind and inviting me in."

Slowly, as carefully as if he were taking a dreadful risk himself, he pressed a kiss to her mouth. His fingers slid into her hair, cupping her head.

But when she tried to kiss him back, he pulled away. "Did you guess what green satin would do to me?" He was smiling when he moved his hands to the first button on her pajamas. The light, teasing brush of his fingers as he slowly pushed the button through the buttonhole sent little shards of feeling through her, bright and sharp. "You're very enticing in satin," he murmured, his fingers sliding to the next button. "But I think you'll be even more beautiful out of it."

His gaze held hers. His fingers moved with painstaking care. They weren't touching her now, just that button and the fabric enclosing it, but as he unfastened it, his knuckles skimmed the side of one of her breasts—just once. Her nipples hardened with longing. But he didn't touch her. Only the satin did, shifting across her sensitive skin as, one by one, the buttons were released.

Then, slowly, he took the edges of her pajama shirt and opened it. And he stopped looking at her face. She heard his sharp intake of breath. "I've never seen you naked," he said. "I want you naked tonight, Jane. I want to see everything."

Her knees went weak, and she began to throb for him, down low. "You, too," she said, meaning that she'd never seen his body, either, and she wanted to. Needed to. Not feeling coherent enough to explain, needing the heat and reassurance of his bare flesh, she reached up and pushed his jacket from his shoulders. He let her do that, but then he caught her hands before she could start on his buttons.

"You have such lovely breasts. So round and pretty." He let go of her hands and moved his to cup her breasts, lifting them. He passed his thumbs across their peaks.

She shivered in delight. "Are you ever going to kiss me?" she whispered.

He shuddered. She felt the tremor pass through him, the physical evidence of some strong emotion. Then his mouth came down on hers.

The world tilted. She grabbed on to him and held on. Colors bloomed behind her closed lids and spun through her body as her neck bent beneath the force of his kiss—bright colors, hot and keen with life. His tongue swept into her mouth as his arms swept beneath her, lifting her off her feet. He stood there with her in his arms, unmoving, his mouth eating at hers as if he needed, wanted, nothing more than this joining of their mouths and breath.

Then he moved, taking the few steps to the bed. His lips didn't leave hers.

Her mind spiralled away into some never-never land of hope and fearful need. It was just as well. Her body knew no doubts. It was eager and avid as he followed her down onto the bed. She pulled at his shirt, hungering to feel his flesh beneath her hands, and fumbled the buttons open while his kiss drove her wild.

He broke the kiss to look into her face. His eyes glittered and his lips were damp from hers when he slid his hands beneath the elastic waist of her pajamas. She lifted herself so he could pull them down and off in one quick motion. Then he was kissing her everywhere, his mouth hot and urgent as his hands sped over her stomach and up to her breasts, where they lingered for a moment. Then, restlessly, they moved lower and lower, until his fingers found the place between her legs where her body pulsed for him.

He shuddered and pulled his head up, staring into her eyes.

"Take off your shirt," he said, even as he parted her with one long finger. "Take it off. I want you to be completely naked this time."

It didn't occur to her to deny him. She squirmed, getting rid of the pajama top while his finger worked magic, stroking, gliding back and forth.

He bent. This time it was her breast he took, not her mouth. He pressed one gentle kiss to her nipple, then another, before taking it fully into his mouth and sucking. She cried out. His finger slid up and down the damp folds of her flesh, driving her crazy, circling without quite touching the spot where she needed to be touched.

She grabbed his shirt. "I want this gone." She pulled at it, and he shifted, letting her yank it down. He pulled his arms out of the sleeves, sucking on her nipple the whole time. She tossed the shirt away and reached for the snap on his jeans.

Getting those off took more effort than it should have. She had to see, to touch, every inch of him. When she did, he went crazy, pressing her deep into the mattress, kissing her wildly. Finally, though, he was as naked as she. He moved between her legs, and she opened them—she was more than ready. But instead of doing what she expected, he kissed the inside of her thigh. Her flesh quivered.

"Samuel," she said, meaning, *Now. I want you now.*

"So pretty," he murmured, and pressed a kiss to her other thigh—a kiss so gentle, in such stark contrast to the need that tightened every muscle of his body, that she fell in love with him all over again. And finally he moved upward, spreading her legs wider with his hands, and rubbed his erection against her.

And then, right at her entrance, he stopped. His hands were on her thighs, his eyes were hard and wild. "I need to know," he said hoarsely. "Why did you change your mind tonight? Why did you ask me into your bedroom?"

Because I love you. The words almost forced themselves out. Almost. Loving him as she did, she had to give him what he wanted: a home, a family, a place to belong—herself. But something kept the words inside, though whether it was fear or wisdom, she couldn't tell. She ran her hands up his chest, feeling the beat of his heart, as frantic as her own. "You're worth the risk," she told him, adding softly, "Come inside, Samuel."

And then, boldly, she reached around to the back of his head, feeling for the thong binding his hair back. She pulled on it even as his body moved. His hair fell loose around his face at the same moment he pushed inside her.

He groaned. The feel of him—large and hot and solid— was perfect. She wanted to stop time, to keep that moment forever, but then he moved in one long, slow stroke, and that was even more wonderful. He thrust again and yet again, and her body, willful and eager, bucked beneath him, demanding more. Harder. Faster.

And he answered—quick and hard and fast. And she met him thrust for thrust, determined on surrender—his, hers, she didn't know or care; the surrender to this driving need was all that mattered—until he gave a hoarse shout. Her body bucked one final time as the universe collapsed around her.

Much later, in the darkness at the middle of the night, she held him. They'd made love a second time with the lights out, and had managed to go more slowly. Making love in the dark had focused her senses more keenly on the touch, taste and smell of him, and she'd loved that slow, intense mating.

But she was glad they'd left the light on the first time. Samuel had spent too much of his life in the darkness.

She thought he was asleep now, with his body curved around hers. His breathing was even and slow, and he didn't move or speak. She couldn't be sure, though. He was still so much of a mystery to her. Maybe he was awake, but content to let her stroke his back quietly. Maybe he liked being held and touched.

He had wanted her. Very much. She hugged that knowledge to herself, even as she hugged the secret of her love for him. Samuel had truly wanted her, and that was surely enough. She knew he might never be able to speak words of love. She told herself that she accepted that. He would marry her, stay with her, because she was having his child. Because he wanted her. Because she could give him the home and family he craved.

Knowing that he would stay was enough.

It would have to be, wouldn't it?

Everything was falling into place. Samuel felt a deep sense of satisfaction when he pulled into the driveway on Tuesday evening. Jane wasn't home yet, but that was okay. She'd told him the committee meeting might run late. There were a lot of last-minute details to be taken care of for the ball on Friday. Jane wasn't in charge of that, but as secretary for the organization that was putting it on, she had to attend all the meetings and send out notices.

He was glad he'd gotten here first today. He wanted to set things up properly before she arrived.

Samuel felt another burst of satisfaction when he put his key in the door. Jane had given him her spare key on Sunday. She wasn't planning to kick him out anymore.

The satisfaction was troubled by a flicker of memory. He'd been given the keys to other doors, too. So many houses, so many families... Some of his foster families had been pleasant, and had tried to make him feel welcome. Some had been neglectful, and one had been a real nightmare—even worse than the times he'd lived with his birth mother. But all of them, even Betty and Stan, had been temporary. He had never belonged. He'd learned to adapt, to control what people saw of him on the surface, keeping the parts of him that mattered tucked safely inside, out of sight.

But this was different. He and Jane were making their own family. The proof of that permanence rested safely in her womb. He reminded himself of that as he put away some of the groceries, leaving out what he needed for his stew. Samuel didn't have a lot of culinary skills, but Betty had taught him a few basics. He could put together a good beef stew.

Two hours later, the meat and vegetables were bubbling away on the stove and he was starting on the salad when he heard Jane's key in the door.

"Something smells good," she called.

He heard the door close behind her. "I thought it was my turn to fix a meal for you." He rinsed the lettuce and set it on paper towels to dry.

"Good grief," she said as she entered the kitchen. "You cook, too?" She shook her head, pretending to frown, but her eyes sparkled. "A man who's at home in the kitchen as well as the bedroom. Amazing."

He could tell she felt quite daring about referring to their intimacy that way. Her flushed cheeks charmed him. He turned around so he could greet her properly. Kissing Jane was still not entirely safe, because he never knew when passion would stay at a quietly exciting simmer, and when it would boil over. But it was addictive.

When their lips parted, her arms were around him. She was smiling. "So, what are we having?"

"We can call it *boeuf Bourguignon* if you want to be fancy," he said, reluctantly releasing her so he could get the wineglasses he'd found on the top shelf of her cupboard. "But basically, it's beef stew."

"Well, if it tastes as good as it smells, I just may keep you."

God, he hoped so. "How did your meeting go?"

She made a face. "Most of the discussion was unnecessary. A couple of people are panicking about the weather. The latest long-term forecast predicts a storm on Saturday, and if it blows in early and hard, it might keep a lot of people home. But there's not much the committee can do about that."

"Other than worry out loud." He took out the bottle he'd bought at the grocery store. He'd used wine in the stew, but Jane couldn't have alcohol right now, so he poured them each a glass of sparkling grape juice.

"They're doing a fine job of that." She took the glass, smiling quizzically. "Are we celebrating?"

"I was called in for my first interview at the college today."

She set her glass down and threw her arms around him. "Oh, Samuel, that's wonderful! How did it go? No, that's a dumb question," she said, hugging him. "You wouldn't have poured us a toast if it had gone badly, would you?"

He had automatically circled her with his free arm. He still had his glass in the other hand. This was even better than he'd planned it, he decided. She was warm in his arms, and happy for him. "It went well," he said, his earlier satisfaction returning even stronger than before. "Drink with me?" He raised his glass to her lips.

She took a sip, her eyes meeting his above the rim of the glass.

He turned the glass so that he drank from the place her lips had touched. It was a whimsical gesture. Romantic. He wanted to give her touches of romance tonight. After tasting the sparkling juice, he had to taste her again—just once, quickly. Then he turned around and set his glass down. "There's another interview still. I don't have the job yet."

"You'll do great," she assured him. "You're very impressive when you want to be."

He liked the idea that she thought so. He turned back to the counter to finish the salad.

"Need any help?" she asked.

"You could get out the dressing." And then, though he hadn't planned to bring the subject up, he said, "You've never asked me if I'm qualified for the position."

"You wouldn't have chosen the background you did if you weren't able to carry it off. I may not know everything about you, but I know you aren't stupid."

He divided the torn lettuce neatly into two bowls, and surprised himself again. "I did attend Eugene Lang College for a couple of years." Under another name, and he hadn't graduated from there. The scholarship money had run out, and he'd transferred to a state school to finish his bachelor's degree.

She nodded. "That makes sense. You know enough about the school and some of the students and professors to speak about them knowledgeably."

Why did what she'd said bother him? It was exactly the reasoning he'd used in establishing this identity, so why did he want to argue with her? "I don't have a graduate degree.

I have the knowledge. I've always been interested in history, so I've done the work. But I don't actually have the degree.''

She walked up behind him and laid her hand on his back. ''That bothers you, doesn't it? You wish you really did have the master's degree you're claiming.''

''It doesn't matter.'' He set the knife against the tomato and sliced once, neatly. ''I have the knowledge I'll need.''

''But you don't have the experience of having gone through a graduate-degree program. You know you can fake it. You're good at that. But you're feeling the gap that exists between who you are and who you're claiming to be, and it bothers you.''

''No, it doesn't.'' Where did she get these stupid ideas? He didn't need her to play amateur psychologist. ''I'm used to living under assumed names.''

''But the name you carry now *is* you, in most ways. This is who you have to be. That's what you told me. It only makes sense that it would feel different this time.''

She was right, and he hated it. He didn't like being this visible to her. It made him feel raw. Out of control. ''Why don't you light the candles?'' he said coolly.

For a moment she didn't say anything. He wondered if he'd hurt her. Then he heard her move away, toward the table. ''Candles, too,'' she said cheerfully. ''We are going to celebrate properly, aren't we?'' The raspy sound of a match being struck told him she was doing as he'd asked.

And that was no reason at all to feel guilty. He brought the two bowls of salad over to the table. ''Sit,'' he said. ''I'll bring the rest of it over.''

''I have something to celebrate, too,'' she said shyly as she took her chair. ''I went ahead and signed up for those workshops. The ones on emergency management.''

He relaxed, pleased for her. ''That's great.''

''I don't know why I'm doing this,'' she confessed. ''It's not as if I want a career in disaster relief. I'm happy teach-ing.''

"It sounds like you're uncertain about your objective." He poured the stew carefully into a serving bowl, thinking about that. It was unsettling not to have a clear goal, he knew. "If you have trouble defining your long-term purpose for this training, you might set a short-term goal." He carried the stew over to the table and set it down near her. "You're a teacher. Have you considered teaching courses on emergency preparedness locally? Perhaps through the Red Cross?"

Her mouth fell open. "No. No, I hadn't. Samuel, that's a wonderful idea. I don't know why I didn't— Yes, I do know. People might not think I'm qualified. I've taken a lot of courses, but I've never *done* anything like that."

He could see she was excited about the idea, and that made him feel good. "I've never sacrificed butterflies to the Aztec serpent-god Quetzalcóatl, either, but I think I can teach others what we know about the rites—what they meant to the participants, how they shaped and were shaped by the culture that evolved them."

"Quetzal—" She smiled and shrugged. "I can't even say it. You really do love history, don't you? I shouldn't be surprised," she added casually as she dished out a helping of the stew. "You're interested in roots, obviously, with all your questions about Atherton. And that's what history is about, isn't it? Our common human roots."

For a moment he couldn't breathe. Even his former boss hadn't guessed the reason for Samuel's lifelong interest in history. Patrick was as shrewd and perceptive a person as Samuel had ever met, yet he believed that Samuel's interest in history had arisen from his interest in political science, when in fact it was the other way around.

Jane had summed up his deepest motives in one simple statement.

"This is great," she said, after sampling the stew. "You know, if you ever decide you missed too much by not having that master's degree, you could go for your doctorate, couldn't you?"

He was saved from having to respond when the phone rang
nd she got up to answer. Which was just as well. He had
o idea what he would say. The idea of going back to school
nder his new name—of letting "Samuel Charmaneaux"
vork toward a legitimate degree—had never occurred to him.
Ie'd been so focused on getting established here....

"It's for you," she said, holding out the receiver. "Some-
ne named Patrick."

The phone call wasn't really a surprise; though he hadn't
xpected to get a call from Patrick at any specific time, he'd
nown he would hear from his old boss again. Patrick's re-
uest wasn't a surprise, either—he still hoped to get Samuel
o do "one more little job" for him. What surprised Samuel
vas the twinge he felt when he turned Patrick down.

For a moment, he'd actually wanted to slip back into his
ld life—back into the shadows. It shook him.

"Who was that?" Jane asked quietly after he hung up.

"No one you know." He started to rejoin her at the table,
nen decided it was time to move on to the next part of his
lan for the evening. He went to get the wrapped box from
ne cupboard where he'd stashed it.

"He's from your other life, isn't he?"

"He isn't someone I can discuss with you." Samuel knew
he'd figured out a few things from his end of the conver-
ation, but he was in no mood for questions. He didn't want
o think about Patrick or his past, or the twinge he'd felt when
e'd turned the job down. He crossed the room and set the
ox, wrapped in pretty green-and-yellow paper, in front of
ane. "Never mind about him. This is for you."

She glanced at the box, picked it up, but then just sat there
vith it in her lap, looking up at him. Her eyes were wide
nd troubled. "Do you miss it at all? What you used to do?"

"No." No, he was sure of that, in spite of the tug he'd
elt toward that old life. "I don't want to go back. I want to
o forward. With you." He knelt beside her chair, laying one
and on her thigh. "Aren't you going to open your present?"

Her smile was a bit unsteady, but her fingers were quic enough to tear open the wrapping her friend Liza had s carefully taped in place at the drugstore that afternoon.

"Ohhh…" she said as she lifted out the terry-cloth tedd bear striped in pale pastels.

"It's very soft," he said. "Squeeze the tummy. And th eyes are seamed into the fabric so the baby can't pull ther off and swallow them." When she didn't say anything, b just continued to stare at the teddy bear, he added uncertainly "I know you were having trouble adjusting to the idea of baby, but I thought you'd like this."

"I do." She turned a glowing smile on him. Her eyes wer damp. "I love it. It's funny, but until this moment, when held this little bear, the baby hasn't been real to me. I mear I knew I was pregnant, but I haven't felt like it, especiall since the nausea stopped. But now…" She blinked the tear away, still smiling. "Now I can picture him. He's got you blue eyes."

"No, she has your eyes," he said, taking the toy from he and setting it on the table. "Big eyes, full of wonder." H stood and held out his hand. When she put hers in it, h pulled her to her feet. "And your smile," he murmured, kiss ing the corner of that smile. "Marry me, Jane."

This time he'd gotten it right. He must have, because sh didn't hesitate. She threw her arms around him, hugging hir tight. "Yes. Oh, yes. Samuel, I love you so much."

He didn't move. He didn't think. There was a roaring i his ears that blotted out everything except the words she' just spoken.

"I love you so much."

He had to get inside her.

He grabbed her face, tilted it up and kissed her, hard. Sh made a startled noise. He told himself to slow down, to giv her time.

He couldn't.

She was wearing a soft corduroy dress in a gentle shad

f green, with dark-colored panty hose beneath it. He pushed
p the full skirt of her dress, kissing her, telling her with his
mouth and tongue what he wanted. What he needed. When
e slid his hand inside the waistband of her panty hose, she
vent very still, but she didn't stop him. And when he stroked
er between her legs, testing and arousing, her thighs quiv-
red, then relaxed, and her hands moved to his nape.

She petted him there, murmuring something as if she were
rying to soothe him. It helped, but it wasn't enough.

I love you so much.

His hands trembled when he pushed her panties and panty
ose down her legs. He wanted to say something, to reassure
er, but he had no idea what to say. He knelt and slipped her
hoes off, one at a time, and then pulled the bunched-up
abric down. She put her hand on his back to keep her bal-
nce as she stepped out of her panties and hose.

He straightened. Her eyes were wide and questioning, but
ot frightened. He brushed the hair back from her face and
issed her cheek, the corner of her mouth. Her lips trembled
eneath his.

The table was small and cluttered with dishes. Even if he
nocked the dishes clear, it might not be sturdy enough. The
ounter would be awkward. So he scooped her up, his hands
nder her bottom, and she instinctively understood, wrapping
er legs around him. She felt good, so good, pressed up
gainst him, warm and accepting. He groaned and covered
er mouth with his again.

The couch. He thought he could make it to the couch in
he living room. The first few steps weren't too hard, but then
he wriggled, rubbing herself against him, and he staggered
eneath a fresh wave of urgency and hunger.

Somehow he got her to the couch. He went down on his
nees beside her, then lifted her dress to her waist and pushed
er legs wide, intending to give her time, planning to touch
nd lick and make her ready. But when he pressed his hand
gainst her center and held it there, cupping her firmly, feel-

ing her heat and moist readiness, she shuddered and pushe
against him.

She wanted him, and he had to be inside her.

He moved between her legs and slid a finger into the plac
that waited for him. Her hands fluttered over his shoulder
and back in quick, entreating pats and tugs. She looked ut
terly wild and wanton sprawled there, her legs wide, her eye
hazy with passion and that other feeling—the one that wa
so much more than passion.

I love you so much.

His hands shook as he unzipped his pants and readied him
self.

When he thrust inside her, her hips were already moving
meeting him. The feeling was indescribable. He couldn'
stop, couldn't slow, but pounded himself into her, his thrust
so hard they scooted her body forward. Nothing else ex
isted—only him and her, the driving rhythm that united them
the feelings and the fire that cascaded over and through him

She cried out, and he exploded.

La petite mort, he thought as, moments or years later, h
drifted back into himself, his body lax and heavy atop her
The little death. He'd heard it called that often enough, bu
he'd never lost control so entirely, had never left himself s
far behind that it came as a dim surprise to find he was sti
here. With her.

He'd taken her without a word. She'd been ready physi
cally, but he'd given her little choice. A chill traveled ove
him, stiffening his muscles, and he forced himself to move
propping himself up on one elbow. ''Are you all right?''

''My goodness.'' She was breathless. Dazed. ''You'll hav
to fix dinner more often. The stew was great, but the desser
was *incredible.*''

Relief loosened his muscles. He realized he was grinnin
back at her.

''Samuel,'' she said, and her eyes grew uncertain again a
her hands slid up his back. ''About what I said...''

He wanted to hear the words again; he couldn't stand hearing them. The contradictory needs ripped through him, destroying his ease. *Not yet,* he thought. Not yet. He pressed a kiss to her mouth. "Just my way of getting out of doing the dishes," he said as lightly as he could.

He saw the disappointment and confusion that flashed through her eyes and he knew he'd hurt her, but he couldn't help it. His own confusion was too great.

Late, very late that night, Jane woke the moment she lost the warmth of Samuel's body beside her. Her eyes came open and she stared, unmoving, at the glowing numbers on her clock. It was 1:32 a.m.

He slipped out of bed, ghost-silent in the darkness.

He was trying so hard not to wake her. Just the way he'd tried not to hurt her when she'd told him she loved him—too soon.

The sounds he made as he retrieved his clothes and his shoes were so soft, she heard barely enough to tell her what he was doing. She didn't really hear him leaving the bedroom, though her ears strained for every sound; she just felt his absence. And when, a few minutes later, the front door opened and closed, it made the quietest of sighs.

She threw the covers back and scrambled out of bed.

One of her living-room windows looked out on the side yard, like the door. When she peeked out the curtains there, she didn't see him. The other window offered a view of the sidewalk at the front of the house. That was where she spotted Samuel, doing a quick series of stretches.

Then he took off running.

Jane blinked back the tears that sprang into her eyes.

She hadn't intended to tell him she loved him. The words had just come out. They'd been so comfortable together, sharing important things like plans and goals, as well as the small details of their days. Then he'd given her the teddy bear, and she— Well, she'd just opened up to him. She'd been too

brimful of love to keep the words inside when he'd aske
her to marry him.

The instant she'd spoken, she'd known it was a mistake
It was too soon. Jane didn't know why Samuel was fright
ened by love. She supposed it had something to do with hi
growing up in the foster-care system, but she hadn't neede
the details to know he wasn't ready to hear how she felt.

Like a fool, she'd told him anyway.

Whatever she had expected his reaction to be, though, he'
surprised her. Amazed her. And given her hope. A man didn'
make love to a woman with such all-consuming urgency i
he truly didn't care whether she loved him or not. Surely h
had to feel something powerful for her to have responde
that way.

But now he was running. At 1:32 a.m.

Jane sniffed and wiped her eyes and insisted that it wa
all right, though it didn't feel right at all. Samuel had tol
her something important with the heat of his need, even i
afterward, he'd made it clear he didn't want to talk abou
feelings—hers or his.

And he was going to marry her. She would have time, sh
reminded herself as she trailed slowly back to her empty bed
She would have plenty of time—years, if that was what i
took—to show him that being loved didn't have to be fright
ening.

He would be a good father to their child—the child tha
was only now beginning to seem real to her. And maybe, sh
thought as she snuggled back beneath the covers to wait fo
him, maybe…eventually…he would feel safe enough on
day to fall in love with her, too.

Thirteen

"**W**hat do you mean, I'm not pregnant?"

Dr. Madison didn't look like a gynecologist. He looked like a grandfather—a little chubby, a lot gray, with jowly cheeks and kind eyes. He sat across his desk from her now with his glasses in one hand and his handkerchief in the other, cleaning the lenses. "Just what I said. I'm sorry, Jane. Obviously you want a baby."

Jane couldn't take in what he'd told her, couldn't accept it. "But the test *said* I was pregnant. And my period—it was skimpy, very skimpy. And the nausea..."

"You have a cyst." He put his glasses back on. "Occasionally a cyst can cause nausea, though I suspect that was due to a simple stomach bug. Cysts can also, very rarely, cause your body to produce the hormone that gives a positive result on a home pregnancy test."

"The test said that false positives almost never happen," she insisted. "Not if the procedure is followed correctly."

"It's quite rare, but it does happen. Three years ago I had

another patient who had a false positive on a home pregnancy test, and it took a while to find out why, since the literature doesn't mention cysts. I did some digging, and…''

Jane stopped hearing him.

She had a cyst, not a baby. Her hands went to her stomach and she fought very hard not to cry. Her baby didn't exist.

''…treat you with an oral contraceptive that contains a high dose of estrogen. Often that will cause the cyst to be reabsorbed into the body. You may notice some side effects—water retention, occasional—''

''I have to take a birth-control pill?'' she interrupted, her voice high and unnatural.

''For three months. After that, you're free to try again.'' He gave her a kind, grandfatherly smile. ''It may not have happened when you thought it had, but I found no reason you can't get pregnant. Give it time.''

But she didn't have time. All those days and years she had thought she would have were gone. They'd never really existed. Just like her baby.

''Jane?'' Dr. Madison sounded worried. ''Is your young man with you? I don't think you're in shape to drive home.''

She made an effort to pull herself together. ''No, he—he had an interview.'' Samuel had wanted to come to the doctor's appointment with her, but when the college called him back for the second interview today, she had insisted he go to it.

Samuel. Oh, God, Samuel. He'd wanted this baby so much.

Dr. Madison wanted to call someone for her, but she talked him out of it. She had to be alone. He wouldn't let her leave until he was sure she was calm, so she made herself be calm.

The hiccups started before she'd driven two blocks.

She didn't cry, though she had to blink away moisture several times. She hiccuped, and she mourned a small life that had never been. And she wondered how she was going to tell Samuel.

Did she *have to* tell him?

When she had left for school that morning, the wind had been playful, sending what was left of last winter's dead leaves skidding along the street. She'd listened to the weather report on her way in, and the forecaster had predicted thunderstorms later that night. The wind wasn't playing now. It blew hard and mean, and the sky was dark with storm.

She had something in common with the weather forecaster, she thought miserably. They both had their timing screwed up.

If she didn't tell Samuel, he wouldn't leave.

It seemed so simple, she thought, as she fumbled her key into the door. She wouldn't take the birth-control pills. Dr. Madison had said cysts were rarely dangerous, so she just wouldn't take the pills, and then she could get pregnant for real. As often as she and Samuel made love, surely it wouldn't take that long.

She wanted the blue-eyed baby she'd imagined when she'd held that teddy bear in her hands.

She went straight to the kitchen, without even stopping to hang up her jacket. Her eyes were dry and burning. She filled a glass with water at the tap and started chugging it, trying to make the hiccups go away. She had to have herself under control by the time Samuel got here.

She'd just set the glass on the counter and was breathing a deep, hiccup-free breath when she heard his key in the door. She tensed.

"Jane?" The door closed. "I saw you turn off on Oak, and couldn't get your attention. You must have been in another world."

Slowly she turned and started for the doorway. I can do this, she thought, holding her stomach with one hand because, for the first time in days, she felt nauseous again. I just have to stay calm.

He stood just inside the front door. He was wearing his dark green sweater again, and the wind had freed a strand of hair from his ponytail. He was holding a big bouquet of balloons, and he was smiling.

And there was no way on earth she could deceive him. She must have been insane to even think she could. He had to know. Her lips trembled. "Samuel." She wouldn't cry. She refused to cry.

His smile fled. He let go of the balloons and started for her. "What's wrong?"

"There isn't going to be a baby," she whispered. "We were wrong. The pregnancy test was wrong."

Samuel heard Jane's words; they just didn't make sense. He stood still. "No baby?" But there had to be a baby. The baby was his future. The baby would bind Jane to him. He had it all planned....

"The doctor said I have a cyst. He wants me to take birth-control pills and says we can try later, but we don't have to wait. Do we? We can try now. Can't we, Samuel?"

"Birth-control pills," he repeated numbly. *No baby.* Jane was going to take birth-control pills. She didn't want his baby? But that wasn't what she was saying—something about trying later, or trying now—but there was no baby.

Jane didn't need him now.

From out of nowhere, anger flooded him. "Did you get rid of it?" he demanded, grabbing her arms and giving her a shake. "Did you change your mind and get rid of it?"

She stared at him mutely. Tears filled her eyes.

He dropped his hands, horrified. "I didn't mean... I don't know what I meant." He took two quick steps away, turning his back to her. God, he was losing it. He had to think. He had to be flexible. He'd always been good at changing his plans to meet the unexpected.

But a baby wasn't a plan.

Grief hit him a hammer blow.

"I'm so sorry, Samuel," the woman behind him whispered.

Jane felt sorry for him. She didn't need him now. She was

crying because he'd hurt her. He felt…too much. The emotions sweeping through him were vast and bewildering, and he had no idea what to think, what to do. He wanted to hold on to something, but he didn't know what. He didn't know how.

The phone rang.

Because it was something to do when he had no goal, no plan at all for even the next minute—because it took him into the kitchen, where he didn't have to see Jane's tear-streaked face—he answered it.

Patrick's voice on the other end of the line offered him a direction. The shadows lapped around him as he listened to Patrick's proposal, but now they were soothing. He wanted the grayness; there was so little feeling there.

When he hung up the phone, she was standing in the doorway, hugging her elbows and hiccuping. She'd heard what he'd told Patrick. Her voice was low and steady. "You're leaving."

"For now." Patrick had tickets waiting for him at the Kansas City airport. He'd told Samuel that if he decided to take the job, he just had to drive in and claim the tickets. It would be a quick bit of business, in and out in less than a week. Familiar territory.

"Don't do this."

He wanted her to move out of the doorway. He was afraid to touch her. "I need to think things through. This will give me time."

"You can think here."

"No," he said. "I can't." Jane made him feel too much. How could he think when he was so full of feelings?

She squeezed her eyes closed and moved out of the doorway.

It didn't take him long to put a few things in a suitcase. He'd done it often enough. But he felt an odd reluctance to zip the bag closed. He felt as if he were doing something unalterable, something he could never take back.

Something wrong.

It would just be for a few days, he told himself, impatient with those nebulous feelings that managed to creep in behind the grayness. He wasn't leaving permanently. He had no idea what he would do permanently. This was a temporary measure.

His entire life had been a temporary measure.

He shrugged off the thought and headed for the living room.

"Samuel, don't do this." She stood beside the door, her face stained by tears, but her eyes were dry. "You hated that other life. If—if you can't stay here with me, if that isn't what you want, you still don't have to throw yourself back into the life you left. You can stay in Atherton. You wanted that. You wanted a hometown."

He couldn't explain. This was something to do, and he desperately needed something to do. Something to focus on. Some shadows to hide in. "I'll be back," he told her as he turned the knob and opened the door. Wind swept inside on a fierce gust.

She grabbed the door. "If you won't stay for your own good, then stay for my sake," she said, very quietly. "You know how I feel about you. I—I love you."

He hesitated. He hadn't been able to say anything the other time she'd spoken those words. He'd been trapped by his feelings. From this gray place he'd retreated to, though, it was easier to speak the truth. "I don't even know what that means."

When he left, he closed the door behind him.

Jane's eyes weren't red when her mother called, though she'd been crying for some time. But she had a monumental case of the hiccups.

"The ball?" she said stupidly, in response to her mother's question. Samuel's balloons still bobbed near the ceiling.

Bright, happy balloons. "I don't—*hic*—I hadn't—*hic*—"
She'd forgotten all about the blasted Charity Ball.

Her mother knew what hiccups meant. "What's wrong,
honey?"

Samuel left me. She couldn't say it, couldn't make the
words come out because then it would be real, and some
wretched, sneaky part of her still hoped he would be back,
that the door would open any minute now and he would be
there. He would say it was all a mistake, that he didn't want
to leave. "There was a—*hic*—an emergency. Samuel had to
go."

"Oh, dear. Nothing too terrible, I hope?"

"I don't—*hic*—I can't talk about it."

Her mother may have assumed she was hiccuping too
badly to discuss it, or she may have been too intent on her
own worries to pursue the matter. Whatever the reason, she
didn't ask again. "Well, if he's not going to be able to go
with you, there's no question about it. You have to stay
home. That's what I called about. The weather has turned
really nasty. They've issued a tornado alert."

"They—*hic*—issue a couple dozen tornado alerts at this—
hic—time of year, Mama." And people were counting on
her. She was supposed to act as one of the hostesses.

Of course her mother discounted that, but the tears were
drying on Jane's face as she realized that, deep inside, *she*
was counting on herself, too. She wasn't going to stay home
and stare at the door he'd closed behind him when he left,
hoping it would open again. "No," she said to her mother,
and swallowed the hiccup that tried to erupt. "No, I'm going
to the ball. I have to."

Of course her mother didn't accept that, but Jane didn't
have the patience to argue or explain, and ended the conversation rather abruptly. Besides, she wasn't sure herself why
she had to do this. She had to be there in half an hour. She
had no time to think, no time to consider or question her
decision.

No time for more tears.

First she chugged a glass of water, drowning the last of the hiccups. Then she raced for the bedroom.

Even as she yanked off her clothes and slid on the dress she'd bought last month, though, she was asking herself why she was putting herself through this. The evening was going to be awful. She knew that. Everyone would want to know where Samuel was. What would she tell them?

Jane shook her head as she headed for the bathroom. She had no idea what she would say. She'd just have to think of something.

The dress was long and slinky, a sky-blue silk sheath with slits on both sides. It was sexy and sophisticated and the most daring dress she'd ever owned. She'd bought it just before she'd left on vacation to San Tomás, and she almost started crying again when she looked into the mirror to put on her makeup. She'd so looked forward to Samuel seeing her in it.

No, she told herself sternly. She couldn't cry anymore. Not now. Her eyes were already swollen, even if they weren't red.

"You do what has to be done." Wasn't that what Samuel had said about her? It was as good a definition of courage as any, and Jane was tired of being a coward. Tonight, what she had to do was to go to the ball alone. She'd deal with the curiosity, the sympathy and the heartbreak. Somehow.

Wind and rain lashed the Jeep. The storm had emptied the highway. Only the foolish or the desperate were out tonight.

Samuel kept his speed down to a decent level, in spite of a gnawing need to hurry. Here, in the gray place where he'd lived for so long, reason ruled, and it wasn't reasonable to push the speed limit when the weather was bad.

Was the weather this rough in Atherton? Would Jane be all right driving to the ball, and home again?

Home. He grimaced and pushed those thoughts away, but they kept coming back. As far as he'd driven in the past hour, he didn't seem to have come far enough. He still saw her face, the tears brimming over in her big eyes and leaving their silvery traces on her cheeks.

He'd made her cry.

She would do better without him, he told himself, and punched at the buttons on his CD player, trying to erase his thoughts with music. What good could he be to her now? He would go back after he finished this job because he had told her he would—but not to stay.

Jane didn't need him now. There was no baby. There never had been a baby. Everything he'd been planning and dreaming and feeling had been a lie, a pretense more hollow than any he'd practiced intentionally.

Hadn't it?

He couldn't hear the music over the noise of the storm. Savagely he twisted the volume knob, and the haunting sound of Mangione's trumpet crooning "Lullabye" flooded the Jeep.

The last time he'd listened to that song, Jane had been beside him.

He went rigid. Music built of shadows and sorrow slid through the grayness around him as nothing else could. The notes were pure and complete, each one linked to the next and to the ones that had gone before, building a melody as simple and perfect as the cycle of day into night. And as each note sounded, it destroyed, slicing through every numb barrier to the pain at Samuel's center, opening him and letting the hurt spill out.

God. He had wanted to be linked the way those notes were. To belong.

Then why was he running away?

Understanding struck, sudden and blinding as the lightning that lanced the darkness overhead. He was running, wasn't he? Running, just as he had as a boy—as hard and fast as he could. But he'd learned long ago that he could never truly run away. He'd always ended up back where he'd started.

Was that really what he wanted? Did he have no choice

but to end up back in the shadows, back in the dim pretense of a life that he'd lived for so long—simply because that was what he knew?

But he couldn't go back to Jane, he thought frantically. What could he give her? How would he hold her?

I love you so much.

The words echoed inside him, going deeper than music, deeper than anything ever had.

She loved him. She wanted him to love her back, and he didn't know what love was. Did he?

There on the storm-chased highway, Samuel took the biggest risk of his life. He let the feelings in. All of them. Sharp and wild, beyond reason or control, they claimed him. He clutched the steering wheel and saw Jane's face, ravaged by hurt and tears as she told him there was no baby. He heard her laughter—on the bus in San Tomás, in a swing at the park. His fingers tingled with the feel of her skin, and unnamed colors bloomed at the backs of his eyes—far back, way beyond the shadows.

They weren't comfortable, those colors. They hurt. But they were alive and they were real—the most real thing about him.

He thought one of those colors might be love.

Or maybe all of them were.

Samuel braked carefully on the deserted highway. The roads were slick, and he couldn't afford another mistake. He'd already made the biggest mistake of his life that night. Just as carefully, he turned his car around. He had to go back. Now. Immediately. He'd been wrong, horribly wrong, to leave.

He'd traveled a few miles back when the lonely road began to get to him. He felt a need to connect with others, with a voice, with the sound of the world he'd found in Atherton and then had tried to run away from. He shut off the CD player and turned on the radio, hunting for a station.

He almost missed the deejay's voice, lost in all the static.

The station was some distance away, and the storm outside
was loud. But he heard the word "Atherton" amid the
crackle and hissing. His hand froze on the knob.

"Tornado…" the radio said. And "Several reports, as yet
unconfirmed by…right down the middle of Atherton. The
destruction…"

Jane. Oh, my God. Jane.

There was nothing reasonable about the way Samuel
floored the accelerator.

The rain stopped before he reached Atherton. At first, as
he drove into the outskirts of the town, he saw only normal
storm damage. Limbs down. Shingles blown from roofs.
Scattered debris, but nothing major.

But the center of the town was dark. The center of the
town, where the VFW hall was located. Where the Charity
Ball was to have been held.

The west end, where Jane lived on the second floor of
Frances Ann's house, didn't seem to have been hit. He saw
lights there, at least, and he wanted to think that Jane had
stayed home to nurse her hurt. But he *knew* otherwise. It was
illogical, this terrible certainty of his. As devastated as she
had been when he left, she might have decided not to go to
the blasted ball. But as hard as he tried to hope she'd stayed
home, he couldn't believe that she had.

She always did what she had to do.

As he got closer to the town center, he had to drive slowly.
There was more damage, and more people. He stopped twice
to ask someone about the fate of the VFW hall. But all he
learned was that one or more tornadoes had touched down,
that there was a great deal of destruction, and that the people
he spoke to, who lived outside the damaged areas, were frantic for news of friends or loved ones of their own.

Samuel knew the streets of the little town. He'd studied
them before he'd arrived, and he'd spent days since then
exploring. The first time he hit a roadblock, he backed up

and took another route. But soon he had to leave the Jeep and start walking, still several blocks from his destination.

Before he'd traveled a block, he was running.

He had seen destruction before, but it had mostly been man-made devastation, from bombs or prolonged gunfire. This was different—perhaps because of the terrible capriciousness of the storm. Cars were overturned, or dropped onto lawns. Electric power lines were down. It was very dark, with the sky still covered by clouds. He leaped over a downed tree in the middle of the street, then had to dodge someone's sofa that was sitting right-side up and unscathed. Three houses in a row had been crumpled to kindling; the next one stood, apparently intact. The roof was missing from the one after that.

People were everywhere. Standing around in shock, some of them. Weeping, in many cases. Some were working purposefully. He saw a few in uniform, with high-intensity flashlights—cops, directing the survivors, watching for looters, comforting the injured. Samuel didn't stop to question any of them. The only answer he could bear to hear, none of them could give him.

She had to be all right. She *had* to be. He ran on, pushing for more speed.

Flames licked at what remained of one building. He saw two firefighters there with a single tank truck. The city's emergency-response people were undoubtedly spread very thin tonight.

He ran faster.

When he rounded the corner of the block where the VFW hall was located, he saw light. He stopped and stared, weak with the first hope he'd felt since he'd heard that radio announcement.

The building stood. It was windowless and intact. Light spilled from the open double doors with a dim glow, not the usual brightness of artificial lighting. Some sort of emergency power, he realized. Light also came from several flashlights held by people in the crowd.

There were a *lot* of people here.

He reached the crowd in front of the hall at a run, but then had to slow to a walk. There were too many people. How could he find one small woman among this number? He spotted someone with a flashlight at the edge of the crowd, a brawny older man with a handlebar mustache. He wore a tie with his white dress shirt—and a brassard across it that bore the familiar emblem of the Red Cross.

Samuel made his way to the man. "I have to find someone," he said tersely. "She was here, and I have to find her."

"You've come to the right place, then. This is where we're collecting names, as well as triaging the injured and putting a roof over the heads of those who don't know where to go. You say the person you're looking for was here? Do you mean at the ball?" When Samuel nodded, he smiled reassuringly. "Then she should be all right. Everyone who was inside made it through okay." He chuckled. "Just as well, since Jane has put us all to work."

"'Jane'?" Samuel wasn't sure if he'd said her name, or just thought it. His heart was pounding too loudly.

"Jane Smith." The man gave him a searching look, then nodded at the open doors. "She'll be right up there at the front somewhere."

There were more people knotted around the doors than anywhere else. Some were crying. Some had children. Samuel picked his way through carefully.

And Jane was there, standing next to the entrance. When he saw her he stopped, still several feet away.

The dim light from inside spilled over her. She was wearing a long, slim column of an evening dress and holding a clipboard. A walkie-talkie dangled on a strap from her wrist. Her hair was a mess. There was dirt on her cheek and on her pretty gown. While he watched, she smiled reassuringly at an older couple and directed them inside the building, then bent to hug a little girl before turning to answer a question someone else asked.

She was alive. She was unhurt and whole. He stood there without moving, without thinking, drinking in the sight of her and tasting the colors that swirled through him—a vast array of emotions he didn't try to put a name to. Jane was alive…and, he thought, smiling slowly, from the look of things, she was in charge.

He didn't know why she looked up just then; he hadn't moved or spoken, and there were people all around her trying to get her attention. But she glanced up from her clipboard and looked straight at him. Her eyes opened wide in shock.

He started toward her, his eyes never leaving her.

As he eased closer, he could tell that some of the people around Jane were volunteers asking for instructions, while others were desperately seeking people who might have been in the path of the tornado. Just before he reached her, she turned to help a limping woman inside the hall.

When Jane came out again, he was there.

She stared up at him, her eyes haunted and her lips pale. "You came back," she whispered.

"Yes." He wanted to touch her. He wanted, very badly, to hold her, but he'd given up the right to do either one when he'd walked out. He had a hundred things to say to her, a hundred things that needed saying, but this wasn't the time or place. "You're all right?" he asked, because he had to hear her say it.

"I—yes," she said. He saw her throat move when she swallowed. "Samuel, I can't—"

"I know. Not now. Where do you need me? What can I do?"

She glanced down at her clipboard, but he wasn't sure if she saw it. There was a blind look to her eyes. "We've got plenty of people inside with the injured, including two of the doctors who were at the ball. You don't have construction experience, so building inspection isn't… But you're strong and sensible." She looked up. "Ben Oakley has a crew on Third. They're clearing the street by hand so emergency vehicles can get through."

"I'll find them," he said. "And later, I'll come back and find you."

Just then another man pushed forward, this one frantic to learn the whereabouts of his mother. Jane directed him inside, where a master list was being compiled from names collected by volunteers in the crowd and by those tending the injured.

When she turned back to him, she said, "I can't talk now."

"I know. There's one thing I have to say before I go find the road crew." He reached deep inside, to the place where the colors lived, and found the courage he needed to give her this gift, whether she still wanted it or not. "My name was Danny."

"Wh-what?"

"Before I was Samuel, I was named Danny." Then he turned and melted away into the crowd.

Dawn was edging out the darkness by the time Jane felt free to take a break. There was still so much to be done, but there were others now to do it. The local Red Cross had been augmented by trained volunteers from as far away as Kansas City. They'd taken over, for now.

All of the injured had been transported. Those who remained were the temporarily homeless, and the men and women who were handing out blankets and food.

Jane sat with her back against the wall of the old brick hall and sipped at the best coffee she'd ever tasted. The place sure looked strange, she thought. The decorations for the Charity Ball were still on the walls, but the floor was crowded with people sitting or sleeping on blankets. She was exhausted enough to curl up on one of those blankets herself. The trauma and demands of the night she'd just passed had left her numb, too tired for the moment to even make her way home.

She was one of the lucky ones. She still had a home to go to.

An hour ago they'd gotten phone service partially restored, and she'd talked briefly to her mother, who had been tearful and overwhelmed. But Jane didn't feel guilty for not taking more time to reassure her mother. Others needed to use the phone, and Marilee Smith had Cherry and the children with her. Jane knew she could count on her sister-in-law to take care of her mother.

Jane took another sip of the wonderful coffee.

She could have caffeine now. She wasn't pregnant.

Apparently she wasn't entirely numb, either. She squeezed her eyes closed against the ache of loss and leaned her head against the wall. She wasn't pregnant, but Samuel had come back—because he'd heard about the tornado and wanted to help?

"Jane."

She jolted upright, nearly spilling her coffee.

His hand was on hers, steadying it. "Don't burn yourself."

"Samuel." She stared at him. He was crouched down next to her, a half smile on his mouth, his hair pulled back as neatly as ever. And he was filthy. "What happened to you?"

"We had to do some digging." He didn't explain further, but held out his other hand. "You need to go home, Jane. You're exhausted."

She let him pull her to her feet, but all the numbness had melted away the moment she heard his voice. "You came back."

He nodded, his eyes serious. "I've got my Jeep out front. Come on. You're too tired to walk."

"Only emergency vehicles are supposed to be here."

He put his arm around her waist, urging her forward. "After we got a couple of the streets cleared, the Cherokee made a decent emergency vehicle. I've been ferrying people and supplies around for the last couple of hours."

She blinked when she reached the door. The early-morning

light seemed very bright after so many hours spent in the dim emergency illumination at the hall. And sure enough, there was Samuel's black Cherokee, right out front. A white placard with the Red Cross emblem rested against the windshield.

The devastation looked worse by daylight. She shivered.

"It looks bad, but this is the worst-hit area," Samuel said quietly. "So far, there's been no loss of life. The old man we dug out of what was left of his house is in critical condition, but none of the others are."

Jane nodded. She knew that, but looking at the debris that had once been people's homes was still hard. And her trees, her beautiful old trees on Second Street—several of them were down. It was stupid to mourn for trees when people were hurt, homeless and frightened. But she did.

They didn't speak as they got into the Jeep. Jane leaned her head against the headrest and closed her eyes—partly because she was exhausted, partly because she didn't want to see the destruction around her...but mostly because of the man beside her.

He'd come back—but he'd also left her, and she didn't know how to feel.

She kept her eyes closed the whole way. She must have dozed a little, because she came awake when he said quietly, "You're home."

Jane got out of the Jeep slowly and looked around. It all looked so blessedly normal that her eyes filled with tears. Some branches were down and the gardens were a mess, but the house was undamaged. "I wonder..." Her voice was so husky she had to stop and clear her throat.

"What do you wonder?" He came around the Jeep and stood in front of her.

"If you hadn't cut that dead limb off the elm out front last weekend, it might have ended up in my kitchen, just like you said." He hadn't done that as part of his "role," she thought. He'd done it because it needed to be done. Just like her, last night.

"Maybe." He took a step closer. "Jane, we need to talk."

Her breath caught, and she stepped back. "I suppose we do. You came back." Her heart beat quick and hard. "I need to know why. Were you planning to just move in with me again, like nothing happened?"

He stood motionless. "I know I can't do that. I screwed up too badly. I should have been here. I should have been with you when the tornado hit."

"Yes." Her hands clenched. "Yes, you should have been here."

"I knew I'd made a mistake. I was on my way back to you when I heard about the tornado, and I—I was terrified."

He had told her his name, she thought. His secret name, the one he'd been born with. The one he'd said didn't exist anymore. He'd come back to her, had already been on his way back when he'd heard about the tornado. The feeling that dawned inside her was strong and quiet—a round, red-orange ball of hope as silent and powerful as the rising sun.

Samuel cared for her. Deeply. Powerfully. She believed that, but she needed to hear the words. She truly needed them. When he moved toward her this time, she didn't retreat, but tilted her head and asked again, "Why did you come back?"

"Because I—" He stopped. Swallowed. "I thought I knew what to say. I thought I had things figured out. I don't. I don't know the right words, and I don't have much to offer you except myself, and I'm not always sure who that is. But I want you more than anything. Take me back. Please."

The warmth from that ball of hope rose in her, flooding her with new energy. With courage. She whispered, "Did you figure out what love is?"

"Oh, yes," he said, his voice soft and certain now. "I know that much. Love is *you*, Jane."

With a cry, she flung herself into his arms. He grabbed her and held on tight, so tight. She was crying—or maybe laughing—and he was pressing kisses to the top of her head, her cheek, wherever his mouth landed.

"I'll give you babies," he promised, kissing her throat. "Our own, if we can have them, or babies that started out with someone else. I don't know if I can be a good husband. I ran away once, and you have to wonder if I'll do that again. I won't—not physically—but I might pull inside myself sometimes. I wish I could tell you I wouldn't, but I've done that too long. I don't know if I can stop altogether."

"It doesn't matter." She grabbed his face and held it still so she could look into the bright beauty of his blue eyes. He wasn't Danny anymore, she realized. But she thought she saw, deep inside, the remnants of the boy he'd once been. "You love me, right?"

"I...love you."

The words had a hesitant quality, as if he were speaking a language new to him. She wondered if he'd ever said them before to anyone. And she ached with such hope and happiness for herself, with such hurt for the bleakness of his life, she thought she would burst. "And if you go away inside yourself sometimes, you'll come back."

"I'll always come back to you, Jane." This time he sounded certain. "When I run, I always end up back where I started. And you're the place where I start, the one thing I want to always come back to."

She stood on tiptoe so she could kiss him once, softly, on the mouth. "Then welcome home, Samuel."

*   *   *   *   *

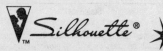

If you enjoyed what you just read,
then we've got an offer you can't resist!

Take 2 bestselling
love stories FREE!

Plus get a FREE surprise gift!

///////////////////////////////////////

Clip this page and mail it to Silhouette Reader Service™

IN U.S.A.	IN CANADA
3010 Walden Ave.	P.O. Box 609
P.O. Box 1867	Fort Erie, Ontario
Buffalo, N.Y. 14240-1867	L2A 5X3

YES! Please send me 2 free Silhouette Desire® novels and my free surprise gift. Then send me 6 brand-new novels every month, which I will receive months before they're available in stores. In the U.S.A., bill me at the bargain price of $3.12 plus 25¢ delivery per book and applicable sales tax, if any*. In Canada, bill me at the bargain price of $3.49 plus 25¢ delivery per book and applicable taxes**. That's the complete price and a savings of over 10% off the cover prices—what a great deal! I understand that accepting the 2 free books and gift places me under no obligation ever to buy any books. I can always return a shipment and cancel at any time. Even if I never buy another book from Silhouette, the 2 free books and gift are mine to keep forever. So why not take us up on our invitation. You'll be glad you did!

225 SEN CNFA
326 SEN CNFC

_____

Name   (PLEASE PRINT)

_____

Address   Apt.#

_____

City   State/Prov.   Zip/Postal Code

* Terms and prices subject to change without notice. Sales tax applicable in N.Y.
** Canadian residents will be charged applicable provincial taxes and GST.
   All orders subject to approval. Offer limited to one per household.
   ® are registered trademarks of Harlequin Enterprises Limited.

DES99   ©1998 Harlequin Enterprises Limited

THE FORTUNES OF TEXAS

*Membership in this family has its privileges
...and its price.
But what a fortune can't buy,
a true-bred Texas love is sure to bring!*

Coming in October 1999...

The Baby Pursuit

by

LAURIE PAIGE

When the newest Fortune heir was kidnapped, the
prominent family turned to Devin Kincaid to find the
missing baby. The dedicated FBI agent never expected
his investigation might lead him to the altar with
society princess Vanessa Fortune....

THE FORTUNES OF TEXAS continues with
Expecting... In Texas by **Marie Ferrarella**,
available in November 1999 from
Silhouette Books.

Available at your favorite retail outlet.

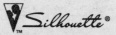

SILHOUETTE BOOKS
is proud to announce the arrival of

THE BABY OF THE MONTH CLUB:

the latest installment of author
Marie Ferrarella's
popular miniseries.

When pregnant Juliette St. Claire met Gabriel Saldana than she discovered he wasn't the struggling artist he claimed to be. An undercover agent, Gabriel had been sent to Juliette's gallery to nab his prime suspect: Juliette herself. But when he discovered her innocence, would he win back Juliette's heart and convince her that he was the daddy her baby needed?

Don't miss Juliette's induction into
THE BABY OF THE MONTH CLUB
in September 1999.
Available at your favorite retail outlet.

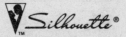

In September 1999 prepare to be

DAZZLED!

by

ANN MAJOR

This new three-book collection by Ann Major will mesmerize you with its glittering locations and dazzling couples.

Lose yourself in three powerfully seductive relationships that radiate off the page with passion.

See what the heat is all about.

Available wherever Harlequin and Silhouette books are sold.

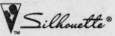

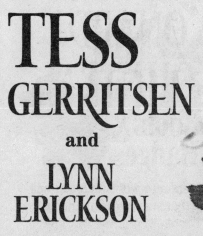